# Upside Down
### and
# Backwards

A Sibling's Journey
Through Childhood Cancer

Published by
MAGINATION PRESS
An Educational Publishing Foundation Book
American Psychological Association
750 First Street, NE
Washington, DC 20002
For more information about our books, including a complete catalog, please write to us, call 1-800-374-2721, or visit our website at www.apa.org/pubs/magination.

Printed by Lake Book Manufacturing, Inc., Melrose Park, IL

Cover and book design by Sandra Kimbell
Cover photos: photo of boy © istock.com/ozdigital;
photo of roller coaster by ENGLISH/RelaXimages/Getty Images
Peach Fuzz font by Typadelic

Library of Congress Cataloging-in-Publication Data
Greves, Julie.
Upside down and backwards : a sibling's journey through childhood cancer / by Julie Greves, CCLS, Katy Tenhulzen, CCLS, and Fred Wilkinson, LICSW.
pages cm
"American Psychological Association."
"An Educational Publishing Foundation Book."
Summary: Follows eighth-grader Bryce as he learns about his sister Paige's cancer and watches his family's focus turn toward her, leaving him feeling left out, jealous, worried, afraid, and confused about the disease. Includes note to readers.
ISBN 978-1-4338-1637-6 (hardcover) — ISBN 1-4338-1637-7 (hardcover) — ISBN 978-1-4338-1638-3 (pbk.) — ISBN 1-4338-1638-5 (pbk.) [1. Cancer—Fiction. 2. Sick—Fiction. 3. Brothers and sisters—Fiction. 4. Family life—Fiction.]
I. Tenhulzen, Katy. II. Wilkinson, Fred. III. Title.
PZ7.G8638Ups 2013
[Fic]—dc23
2013020711

Manufactured in the United States of America
First printing October 2013
10 9 8 7 6 5 4 3 2 1

# Upside Down and Backwards

## and

## Backwards

## A Sibling's Journey
## Through Childhood Cancer

by Julie Greves, CCLS, Katy Tenhulzen, CCLS,
and Fred Wilkinson, LICSW

Magination Press • Washington, DC
American Psychological Association

# Contents

# Prologue

Ever since my first ride, I have been obsessed with roller coasters. There is something about the "hiss" of the ride starting that fills me with anticipation. I love looking out at the park during that initial slow ascent—leaning back, staring at the sky while the cars climb slowly up the track, clicking as the guide wheels make their way up that first steep hill. Everything seems to get smaller and smaller as the car climbs higher. I look down at the people on the ground, happily going about their day, paying no attention to me sitting several hundred feet up in the air, heart pounding, about to careen over a steep drop. The car pauses at the peak of the hill just long enough for my adrenaline to build.

Then comes the plunge.

The wind whips my face so it feels like my cheeks are being stretched back into my ears, and I don't know whether to laugh or scream. Throughout the whole ride I hold on for dear life, stomach in my throat, screaming my head off, until the cars gradually come to a stop with another familiar "hiss."

Waiting in line to get on, I always watch the people who have just finished the ride. The cars pull up, full of passengers with red faces and hair going every which way. Some smile and laugh, while others stand up with shaky legs and this shocked, nauseated look on their face, as if they are thinking, "I can't believe I survived that." I always feel bad for the ones who look so miserable when they get off. I love the adrenaline, but if you don't, it sure would suck to be stuck on the ride, panicking that it's taking you on unpredictable twists and turns at lightning speed when all you want is to have two feet steadily back on the ground. I guess some people just don't really know what they are getting themselves into. The ride looks less scary when you're watching from the ground, but for some, once they are the ones getting flipped upside down and backwards, it's not as much fun as they thought it would be.

Little did I know that in the spring of my eighth grade year my sister Paige would be diagnosed with cancer and my life would become one of the craziest roller coasters I would ever ride. As much as I love roller coasters, this was one I definitely did not climb on by choice. There were many, many times when I just wanted my two feet safely back on solid, predictable ground. But I was buckled into my seat, and there was no getting off once the "cancer coaster" started—I just had to hold on as my life flipped upside down and backwards.

# Chapter 1

# The Screamroller

The car moved in slow motion up the track—*click, click, click, click.* I felt a flutter of anticipation and excitement in my stomach as we got closer to the top. For a moment everything stopped as we reached the highest point. Then a collective scream rang out as we plunged down, down, down. Right when we reached the bottom, the track curved back up and took the car around and upside down. My stomach flopped up into my throat and then dropped along with the car, heavy in my gut. After two more loops, I couldn't figure out which way was up. Finally the car slowed as it reached the end of the ride.

"Woo hoo!" my best friend Tyson hollered as he stepped off. "We conquered the Screamroller!" He started punching the air like Rocky Balboa. I followed him more slowly, laughing, my legs feeling slightly wobbly. I did my best to seem chill as Kelsey and Rebecca stepped off the car behind us. Becca, always concerned with looking her best, was smoothing out her hair. Kelsey, on the other hand, didn't appear to notice or care that her long blond hair was tangled and a few strands were almost standing on end. I always appreciated how low-maintenance Kelsey was. It was the last day of spring break and we were at the local amusement park to distract us from the reality facing us the next day. We all headed over to the designated meeting place where Luis and Jamal were already digging into sugar-coated elephant ears. I breathed in the smells of cinnamon and butter and was glad I'd waited until after the ride to get one for myself, unsure if it would still be in my stomach if I hadn't.

Ty and I always talked about taking a long road trip someday to visit all the best roller coasters across the country. I laughed to myself as I stood in the concession line, thinking back to the first time he made me go on one. We were eight. I didn't want to admit it to Ty, who never seemed fazed by anything, but I was scared out of my mind as I watched the cars looping and zooming around, listening to the screams of people hanging upside down in the loops. I could barely breathe through the first half of the ride, but on the way down, screaming like a wild man, I realized that the rush of speed was addictive, and I felt proud of myself for conquering it.

I felt an elbow jab me in the side, interrupting my thoughts. Kelsey had a big smile on her face as she teased, "Earth to Bryce!" I suddenly noticed I was next in line.

"Three elephant ears, please." I handed my money over to the vendor and gave one of the hot pastries to Kelsey, who smiled even bigger as she took a huge bite out of hers before we even started walking away. Yet another reason to appreciate that girl: she ate anything and everything. Becca, on the other hand, scrunched up her nose at us and said, "I can't imagine how many calories are in one of those things."

As I handed Tyson his, he rolled his eyes and declared, "Oh Becca, you let little things like calories ruin all the joys of life! All this sugary goodness hot out of the fryer, mmm-mmm!"

Jamal, being the Eeyore of the group, broke the relaxed mood by mentioning the "S" word. "School tomorrow and a test the first day back. Did anyone study this week?"

Luis threw his wrapper at him. "Dude, seriously, that topic is off limits until about 8 o'clock tonight. We still have hours of vacation left before we need to stress about that!"

## Chapter 2

# The Calm Before the Ride

When I got home, I smelled the spaghetti sauce before I even opened the front door, and headed straight into the kitchen. Dad was standing at the stove stirring the sauce and smiled as I walked in. "How was it?" he asked as I grabbed a bottle of water out of the fridge.

"Awesome! We rode the Screamroller! It was crazy, but so much fun." I sat down on a stool at the kitchen counter as our English bulldog, Zeke, walked up to greet me, sniffing my pant leg. He looked up at me with accusing eyes, apparently catching a whiff of some grease from a treat he wished I'd brought home for him. His wrinkled face, under-bite, and grumpy scowl made me laugh. I scratched his head for a minute until I was apparently forgiven and he curled up by my feet.

"Are you hungry for dinner or is your stomach still doing flip flops?"

"I'm down for some spaghetti. When will dinner be ready?" I didn't want to mention I wasn't all that hungry since I had eaten that gigantic elephant ear; I knew Dad would be annoyed that I had eaten junk that close to dinner. As I saw him chopping up some garlic and brushing olive oil on some bread, I figured I'd be ready to dig in by the time we sat down to eat.

"Should be about a half hour. Your mom and Paige went to a movie. They should be home any minute."

"I thought Paige was going to the mall with her friends."

"She was supposed to, but she wasn't feeling all that great. So she just wanted to do something low-key instead."

I noticed Zeke sniffing at my other pant leg and thought maybe I should change before he started gnawing on my jeans. "Oh, okay. I'm going to jump in the shower. I'll be down in a few."

I took the stairs two at a time. I stripped off my clothes while the water warmed up, and caught my reflection in the mirror. My shaggy, stick-straight hair jutted out in several directions—a side effect of the roller coasters earlier today. I attempted to flatten a particularly messy patch only to have it spring right back up again when I moved my hand.

I took a hurried shower knowing that dinner would be on the table soon. Wiping the steamy mirror with my hand, I glanced at my reflection again, now free of all evidence of my crazy day.

"Bryce, dinner's ready!"

"Coming!" I yelled as I pulled my favorite hoodie over my head.

I ran downstairs and walked in to hear my sister telling my dad about the movie as she helped set the table. "It was hilarious!" She turned to me. "Bryce, you and Ty *have* to go see it." Paige smiled as she laid the last fork down on the table. "I laughed so hard my stomach hurt. You should have come with us!"

My mom had just pulled a pitcher of iced tea out of the fridge but managed to reach out and wrap her other arm around my shoulder, giving me a kiss on the head with a smile. I grabbed the pitcher from her and set it on the table as I sat down. Dad placed a steaming bowl of spaghetti on the table and turned to finish tossing the salad. "I'm impressed you stayed awake through the whole thing. You were so tired this morning."

"Everyone in the theater was laughing so hard. Nobody could have slept through that." She grabbed a slice of carrot out of the salad bowl as Dad placed it on the table and sat down. "Hey, Bryce, how was the park?"

"Awesome! We got to ride most of the coasters at least twice. The Scream-roller was amazing. It took us upside down twice and it was so fast."

Not a big fan of crazy rides, Paige laughed and shook her head. "Sounds great—if you enjoy feeling like you're going to fall out of the sky. Was Kelsey there?" Paige plopped down in her chair with a sly grin. I turned to her and gave her a look as I helped myself to a slice of garlic bread.

"And who is this Kelsey?" Dad asked, giving me a half smile, a sparkle in his eye.

"Just a friend from school." I could feel my face getting flushed. Time to change the subject...quickly. "Did you hear what happened in spring training today?"

When in doubt, talk about baseball.

## Chapter 3

# Just Another Day

We were all a little late getting going Monday morning. I hit the snooze button one too many times. Paige spent even longer than usual in the bathroom figuring out her perfect ensemble while complaining about how tired she was. I went into the bathroom to brush my teeth and shook my head at the skirt and three shirts strewn on the floor and the assortment of hair clips and bands scattered on the counter by the sink. All that effort to look fashionable, and she wasn't even going to school that morning because of a doctor's appointment.

We were all quiet on the ride to school. I looked out my window as we passed by the familiar homes. Science test today. We had a few unexpected snow days in February, so I guess Ms. Reynolds felt like we were behind and had to jump right back into reality straight away. Brutal to have a test the first day after break! Tests stressed me out. How is it I can remember things perfectly until I actually have to write them down to prove that I know them? I recited the parts of a cell in my head. *Cytoplasm, nucleus, nucleolus...* I was so focused I barely noticed that the car had stopped and we had arrived at school.

"Bye, Bryce, have a good day!" Mom leaned over to kiss my head.

I grabbed my bag and reached for the door handle to climb out. "See you later! Have 'fun' at the doctor, Paige!" I said with a hint of sarcasm. I turned to wave as Paige stuck her tongue out at me and slid into the front seat I'd just left.

I stopped at the office to drop off a note from Mom excusing Paige's absence, and slipped into my homeroom desk just seconds before the bell rang.

The day started like any other day, but I felt sluggish coming back after the break. First period math was always rough since numbers are not my brain's forte. At least I would get the worst over with early.

Mrs. Mitchell, cheery morning person that she was, smiled brightly and said, "All right, guys! Books closed, pencils out. Time to wake those brains up!"

You have got to be kidding me. A pop quiz on the first day back?

I shifted in my chair as I slid my book on top of my backpack under my desk. The day before break started I had gotten back a test that was a few letters too far below an A. What was it with teachers wanting to jump right back in after vacation? Maybe this was only to shock us back into reality and the grade wouldn't count. I could only hope.

After writing my name at the top of the page I took a deep breath and looked at the first problem. *Bob enjoys playing basketball and makes his shot 75% of the time. If he takes 30 shots, how many of them will go in the basket?*

Nice! I smiled to myself and breathed a sigh of relief, thankful that I had done my homework as I started writing out my answer. All three questions on the worksheet involved sports, which was cool. I could deal with math a whole lot better if all of the problems were sports-related. At least I should be getting a better grade on this quiz than I did on the test.

I handed in my paper, reached under my chair to grab my science book from my backpack, and flipped it to the chapter on cells one more time as the last few people finished their math problems. After a lesson given by our much-too-excited-about-numbers teacher, the bell finally rang. Mrs. Mitchell blurted out our homework assignment. I could barely hear her with the rustling of papers and closing of books as we all scrambled to get out of there. The next two classes were basically a repeat of the first—same thing, different teacher—but fortunately there were no more surprise math questions.

I made it through my last class before lunch, then stopped to throw my stuff in my locker and grab my food. As I entered the crowded cafeteria, I looked around for my friends. I heard a loud laugh off to my left and knew without even looking that it was Tyson. He has the loudest and most contagious laugh of anyone I know.

As I walked up to the table, Luis and Jamal scooted over to make room for me. I pulled out my PB&J and opened my bag of chips. Tyson complained, "Aw man...my mom always packs me a turkey sandwich and an apple...can't a guy get some red meat or something?! Cavemen ate real meat, not turkey." He reached for a handful of my chips.

"Hey, caveman! Save some for me. Have you ever thought about packing your own lunch? You're not in kindergarten anymore, you know."

Ty shot me a look, then got a glimmer in his eye and put his hand over his heart. "I can almost smell the hot dogs at Opening Day. Mmm-mmm. I haven't had a hot dog since last season. No turkey sandwiches at the ballpark!" Every spring, our dads took us to Opening Day to kick off baseball season; it had been a tradition for as long as we could remember. We were anxiously counting down to the big day.

"I know....I can hardly wait for a big bag of kettle corn. This is the year I'm going to catch a foul ball. I'm bringing my mitt and it is destined for greatness!"

Tyson rolled his eyes at me. "Yeah, well, you better get out and practice some more, after that fly ball you dropped..." He lightly punched me in the shoulder and I groaned.

"Dude, the sun was in my eyes! And besides, it was just practice. And it was two weeks ago already. Let it go!"

"Yeah, right, or maybe you were too distracted by Kelsey running by."

"Whatever, the track team needs to stick to the track and not do their warm ups all over everyone's fields." I knew my face was a little red but luckily Jamal changed the subject to our upcoming science test, and before I knew it, lunch was over. Why is lunch always the fastest period of the day?

My afternoon classes were more fun, so the time went by way faster than the morning. In art class we made "interpretive self-portraits." We drew the outline of a face and were supposed to cut out magazine pictures or words that define who we are. I spent most of the time flipping through a *Sports Illustrated,* cutting out words like "athletic" and trying to find someone in the magazine that had blue eyes like mine that I could glue on my picture.

I found my seat in science class, and Ms. Reynolds didn't waste any time starting the test. "All right, guys, I'm going to pass out the exam and you'll have the whole period to work on it. Don't forget to put your name on the top. If you finish before the bell, please read quietly at your desk."

I glanced over at Luis who was nervously shaking his knee up and down and twirling his pencil between his fingers. The pencil went flying out of his hand and rolled under my desk. I leaned over to grab it for him and passed it back.

"You okay?"

"Yeah, just thinking I should have studied more."

I reached forward to grab the stack of tests, grabbed mine, and passed the rest to the girl behind me. Just like I do when I step up to the plate to bat, I closed my eyes and took a deep breath. Forty-five minutes later, I was pretty sure I had written down everything I knew about the structure of a cell. The last shriek of the bell and I was out of there. Poor Luis was still frantically trying to fill in the last answers on the cell diagram when I left. I gave him a half-smile as I walked by his desk, but he was writing so fast I don't think he even noticed everyone leaving around him.

I weaved my way through groups of kids walking in all directions to get their stuff ready to go home or to sports practice. I was kind of disappointed we didn't have practice again today, since they were still finishing up some work on the field. I was going to be pretty rusty tomorrow after over a week of no practice.

I hid my laugh as I walked by Jamal trying to look cool talking to a seventh-grade girl but failing miserably. She kept looking past him, probably hoping one of her friends would come by and save her. Finally, I pushed open the heavy, green double doors to the outside.

# Chapter 4

# "Something"

I squinted in the sunlight as I walked outside. I scanned the line of cars for my mom's, but didn't see it. Had she forgotten that practice was canceled? I hoped not; we were supposed to go shopping after school to get some new cleats. I searched the line of cars again. Was that Dad's car? Why would he be here? It was always Mom who picked us up if there was no practice after school.

I glanced over to the bench where Paige and I normally met if we were getting picked up, but it was empty. I guess she didn't end up coming to school. I slowly walked towards the car to see if it was Dad. Sure enough, there he was, staring out his window. I tapped on the passenger side window and Dad jumped as he looked over and then gave me a distracted smile.

What was he doing here? On Mondays we usually didn't see him until later, when we met up for dinner at our favorite Mexican place after I finished practice and Paige finished her dance class. And even then, we'd usually have gone through one whole basket of the warm, salty chips before he showed up apologizing for working late. Mmm, the thought of those chips made my stomach growl.

"Hey, Dad! What are you doing here?" I asked as I hopped into the front seat.

He didn't say anything at first. "Well, Bryce, there's...we need to talk." He had on his serious face as he started to drive. My rumbling stomach dropped as if I'd just stepped off the Screamroller. I suddenly didn't feel quite as hungry as I had a minute earlier.

"Uh, okay." What had I done? I tried to think back. It sure seemed like I was in trouble for something.

Dad interrupted my thoughts. "Your sister went to the doctor today." Oh, so this was about Paige?

"I know. Mom took her after she dropped me off at school. Why, what's wrong?" I felt a little distracted, and started to think about dinner again.

"Well, actually, the doctor found...something...and he is having Paige stay at the hospital to run a few more tests."

*Something?!* I snapped back to reality. What does that mean? It had to be more than "something" if they were going to make her stay in the hospital. My stomach twisted up in knots. What could be so wrong with my sister that she had to stay in the hospital?

"Is she going to be okay?"

"She's okay," Dad said, trying to reassure me. "She is a little scared but Mom is staying with her this afternoon and tonight. Besides, this will give us a chance to have a guys' night." Although he was trying to sound calm, Dad was talking kind of fast.

We didn't really say much for the rest of the drive home. I wished I could take away some of Dad's stress. But I couldn't think of anything to say that didn't sound stupid.

When we got home, I threw my backpack in the corner of the entryway. The house was really quiet without Paige blaring her music or talking on the phone like usual. I wasn't sure what to do with myself, so I headed upstairs to the rec room and slumped on the worn couch. I tried to play a video game to distract myself, but I couldn't really focus on what I was doing, so the zombies kept getting me and I finally gave up.

How could Paige be so sick that she had to stay in the hospital? She had been more tired than usual lately, but I didn't notice that she seemed sick at all. In sixth grade a girl in my class had something called mono that made her really tired all the time, although she hadn't gone to the hospital for it. And everyone teased her because mono is also known as "kissing disease." Paige hadn't been kissing anyone—at least she better not have been. Otherwise I might have to track someone down and have a little talk with him.

Hopefully she would be home tomorrow like nothing had even happened and I could give her a hard time for being overly dramatic. My scattered thoughts were interrupted by the smell of something good cooking downstairs, and I remembered how hungry I was since we'd skipped the Mexican food tonight. My growling stomach made my brain slow down for a bit, and I ran downstairs. Nice—Dad was heating up a frozen pizza. We rarely got to eat that kind of stuff. Except for our Monday night Mexican, Mom and Dad were usually all about home-cooked food. That's great and all, but every now and then you can't beat some gooey, cheesy, pepperoni pizza out of a box.

I grabbed two slices and slid them onto my plate.

"How was school?"

"Pretty good. We had a test in science. Can you believe that? The first day back!"

"That's pretty rough."

"How was your day?"

"Fine, thanks."

Silence....

This is usually the point when Paige would jump in with some gossip or drama happening at school. Considering we go to the same school, it always amazed me the things she heard about that I hadn't. Dad and I have had plenty of meals just the two of us, but the vibe was different tonight. His mind was definitely somewhere else.

I scarfed down my pizza, and was halfway through another slice before I noticed that half of Dad's slice was still left uneaten on his plate.

"Want some ice cream?" asked Dad.

"We have some?" My eyes lit up—we usually didn't have much sugary food in the house.

"Yeah, we have some mint chocolate chip. Aunt Kelly left it behind last time she came for dinner."

"Nice. My favorite. Did she leave any chocolate syrup too?"

"I think so—check the fridge."

"Score!" I grabbed the bottle from the shelf. Got to love Kelly and her sweet tooth.

"Not too much, okay?"

I was stuffed by the time I licked the last of the chocolate from the bottom of the bowl. I leaned back in my chair and tried to think of something to say to break the silence. Dad just kept swirling the green, melted ice cream around in his bowl. It was starting to look more like soup than ice cream. Finally, I gave up.

"Well, I think I'm going to head upstairs and do my homework."

"Okay, just clear your bowl first, please."

After I brought my bowl over to the sink, I trudged upstairs to bury my nose in my books in an attempt to distract myself from the "something" that Paige had.

Our roller coaster ride was beginning. The shoulder restraint had come down, locked into place, and there was no getting off.

# Chapter 5

# Tired

When the shrill beep of my alarm sounded the next morning, I half expected to hear the water running from Paige's shower. Eyes still closed, I fumbled over the alarm clock trying to find the "off" button.

"Ugh. I could use just five more minutes...." I mumbled, as I used all of my willpower to make myself sit up. I knew that if I lay there any longer I would fall asleep again.

I got in the shower, and took a few minutes longer than usual since Paige didn't need to get in to re-do her hair for the tenth time. On my way downstairs I heard the whir of the coffee grinder. I was so tired that for a second, I considered asking my dad for a cup of coffee.

"How'd you sleep?"

"So-so. You look like you didn't sleep great, Dad," I said, glancing at the dark circles under my dad's eyes as he covered a huge yawn with his hand.

"Yeah, definitely not the best night. I'm going to head to the hospital after I drop you off at school. Aunt Kelly will pick you up."

"I have baseball practice today."

"I know, but I really think today it would better if Kelly picked you up right after school so that you guys can come see Paige in the hospital."

"Okay." I was bummed to miss practice, but I did want to see Paige.

I stared out the window during most of the drive to school. Dad was definitely quieter than usual. I could tell his mind was already at the hospital so I didn't even bother trying to make small talk.

"Tell Mom and Paige I say 'hi,'" I said, hopping out of the car.

"Will do. And remember, Aunt Kelly will be picking you up."

"I know, Dad. You told me that already," I said, trying to get out of the car quickly. I caught a glimpse of Kelsey getting out of her mom's car.

"Hey, Kels, wait up!" I caught up to her on the stairs.

"Hey! No Paige today?"

"Nah. She's still not feeling well." I didn't really feel like telling anyone she was in the hospital. I didn't want to deal with the questions that would follow—especially when I didn't have the answers.

"That's too bad. Tell her I hope she feels better soon. I have to get to my locker before class but I'll see you later!"

## Chapter 6

# The "C" Word

After a thankfully uneventful day of school Aunt Kelly picked me up and we headed back to her house. When she parked the car, I hopped out and walked up the steps to the front porch Paige and I jokingly called "the jungle" because it was packed with pots full of flowers in every color of the rainbow, and hanging baskets with vines and leaves hanging down so low I almost had to duck under them to get to the door.

I loved coming to Kelly's house to hang out. She let me get away with things that my parents never would, like playing video games with no time limit and watching more TV in a day than my parents let me watch in a week. Plus, of course, her house was always stocked with sweets. Even though she was my dad's sister, she looked nothing like him, and they were almost complete opposites in every way. Mom calls Kelly "funky." She has a bright butterfly tattoo on her ankle, and always has her hair streaked a different color. Today it was pink. Paige thinks our aunt is so cool and I can tell that kind of freaks Mom out. I think Mom worries that Paige will want a tattoo on her ankle someday, too. But we all love being around Kelly; she is just one of those people who make life more fun.

Kelly's son Max is seven, and she calls him her little "Tasmanian Devil." Picture a whirlwind running around like crazy, pulling things off shelves, and never shutting up. That's Max. He isn't a bad kid, but with so much energy he is exhausting to be around. Max looks like a mini version of my aunt, except no pink hair or tattoo. He had gone to a friend's house after school, so that meant Kelly and I could hang out in peace until we got the call from Dad to head to the hospital.

Kelly and I walked downstairs to Max's rec room. Next to a couple of framed pictures from the book *Where the Wild Things Are,* she had painted letters on the wall that read, "Max's Wreck Room." As I looked around at the mess of Legos, Spider-Man stuff, trucks, and who knows what else, it seemed like a fitting name for the space.

We both just stood there for a second, looking at the chaos but not really focusing on anything in particular. Kelly didn't exude her usual energy as she asked, "What do you feel like doing?"

"I brought some of my video games. Is Max's system hooked up?"

"Right over there. Go for it—you know how to work that thing better than I do." Kelly plopped onto the couch and tucked her feet underneath her.

"I know you aren't a huge fan of war games, but I just got a new one and was hoping to try it out."

As cool as Kelly is, I knew she was beyond "not a huge fan" of violent games—she hated them. She raised one eyebrow and squinted her eyes at me. "How bad is it?"

"Not too bad. You have to try to find the other guys' sniper before he finds you. I've played it at Ty's house a few times; it's really cool."

"Put it in and let's see how it goes."

I handed Kelly a controller and explained the basics. She couldn't even figure out how to change weapons or set up a target. She was pretty terrible, but I had to give her credit for trying.

"Ahhhh, killed again," she moaned. "I give up!" She tossed her controller on the couch. "Do you want me to make you a smoothie or something?"

"That sounds awesome. Banana, chocolate, and peanut butter?"

"Is there a better kind?" Kelly asked with a smile. "Why don't you start your homework while I go whip some up?"

As I cracked open my math book I heard Kelly banging around in the kitchen and turning the blender on. There was a distant ringing sound and I laughed as I heard Kelly's footsteps running in circles, probably looking for her cell phone that she always misplaced.

"Hello?" she answered breathlessly. Things sounded a little mumbled from downstairs, but I picked up a lot of *uh-huhs* and *ohs.* I admit it: I have a bad habit of eavesdropping on people's phone calls. It drives Paige crazy.

Then, through the mumbles, I could have sworn I heard her say the word *cancer.* I could feel my eyes get huge as I mouthed the word back to myself. *Cancer.* Did I hear that right? I suddenly felt a lump at the back of my throat and my stomach sank. Mono. It was supposed to be mono or some other stupid little sickness that everyone overreacted about.

*Cancer.* Seriously?

"I can't believe this. I know, okay, we'll see you tomorrow." Kelly's voice trembled as she was saying goodbye. Should I go upstairs? Part of me wanted to stay in the basement because I knew once I asked the question it would make it real. Taking a deep breath, I slowly walked upstairs. I emerged from the top step to see Kelly quietly crying at the kitchen table.

"Kelly, was that my mom on the phone?"

"Yes, honey, it was," she said, wiping away her tears.

"Does Paige really have cancer?"

Kelly looked right into my eyes. "She does, Bryce. But we don't have a lot of details yet. I wish I knew more..." she trailed off. "You'll stay here tonight, and I'm going to take you to the hospital in the morning, after I drop Max off at school."

"Tomorrow? Can't we go tonight?"

Kelly took a shaky breath. "There is so much going on right now, and they are still dealing with the news..." she wiped her cheek with her sleeve.

I felt tears prick my eyes and wished I could just be with my family, and that we could all be together to deal with the news. There were so many things I wanted to say, but my mind was racing and kept coming back to that word: *cancer.* "Kelly. Is she going to be okay?"

"She's in the best place she could be to treat this. There are a lot of people who will be working hard to help get her better." Kelly hugged me. We sat in silence as we drank our smoothies, although I didn't taste much of mine.

We had to go pick up Max. I stared out the window watching cars and houses as we passed them by. The sun was hot beaming in through the sunroof, and there was a heavy feeling in the car. I rolled down my window to feel the breeze blow over me. Neither of us knew what to say.

If our life was becoming a roller coaster, I guess this was the part of the ride when you feel a little jerk as the car first starts. For the first-timers, this is the sign that the ride has started, you can't get off, and although you don't know what's ahead, you brace yourself for the worst.

Kelly pulled up a steep driveway to a white house with a bright red door. She got out and I watched her go to the front door and knock. Max came bolting out the door and down the porch stairs.

"Brycie!" Max yelled as he climbed in to the back seat. Before I could even reply, he continued, "Hey Bryce, guess what? I was at my friend Charlie's house and it was awesome. We played trucks and Spider-Man and tried to hit each other with a soccer ball while the other one ran across the back yard. And then guess what? His mom let us have cookies, chips, and even a soda for an after-school snack." I don't even think he took a breath. That kid acted like he took an hourly shot of caffeine. He was cute and all, but I felt exhausted just being around him. It was going to be a long night.

## Chapter 7

# The Maze to Room 3296

By the time we dropped Max off at school the next morning I was already exhausted. I zoned out the window on the drive to the hospital, thinking about how Paige was doing.

"Okay, here we are," Kelly said as we pulled into the hospital parking lot. As we walked toward the huge building, I felt my heart start to pound and it was a little hard to breathe. I had no idea what to expect inside, especially once we got to see Paige.

The double doors at the entrance opened with a big *whoosh*. Straight ahead of us was a desk where we stopped to get our visitor badges. We were on our way to stop at the gift shop when a ringing sound came from Kelly's bag.

"You should pick out something cheery for Paige's room, Bryce," Kelly said, as she searched her bag for her phone.

I really wanted to see Paige and my parents, so I grabbed the string of a balloon without looking at it. Kelly paid for it as she talked into her phone. "Okay, well, we're here, so we'll see you in a few."

Kelly and I started going through what seemed like a very complicated maze, turning down hallways and getting on two different elevators. The hallways reminded me of an airport. There were signs overhead telling you what "zone" you were in, and there were arrows pointing in every direction. Finally, we found the zone where Paige's room was. There was a big set of double doors with a sign held up by two painted kangaroos that read "Hematology/Oncology." The animals were cute, but they didn't distract me enough from those words, whatever the heck they meant. I pressed a huge silver button on the wall and the doors slowly opened. I felt like I was entering a spaceship.

"Hi. We're here to see Paige."

The woman sitting at the front desk had a big smile and a name badge that read *Taylor*.

She reached to pick up one of the two phones sitting in front of her on the desk. "Sure, just one second. Let me see if she is taking visitors right now."

She got on the intercom and I heard her say "Paige's family?"

"Yes?" Mom's crackly voice answered.

"Is it okay to send visitors back?"

"Sure!"

What the heck?! A visitor? I'm her *brother*. Of course I could come back! I didn't even knock on her bedroom door at home when I wanted to come in, and now I had to have permission to go see her? Of course, it always made her crazy when I barged into her room; she probably loved this chance to decide whether to "buzz" me in.

Taylor interrupted my thoughts with another big smile as she said, "She's in room 3296. Down this hall and to the left. Go on back!"

I felt the light weight of the balloon trailing behind me as I looked at the room numbers on each door we passed. *3291, 3292...*How many rooms were there?! Some of the doors were wide open and I noticed that the rooms were decorated floor to ceiling with pictures and bright posters. In one room I saw a comforter with big pink and yellow flowers on the bed. It looked like the girl had practically moved in, like she had transferred her whole room from home to the hospital. Other rooms were dark with the shades drawn. I wondered if those rooms just didn't have anyone in them, or if there were really sick kids in there avoiding visitors. I tried my best not to stare in each open door when we walked by, but I wanted to see what was going on inside each room. From what I could see, it wasn't anything too dramatic—mostly kids watching TV or playing games with their parents. It reminded me of when I'd stay home from school sick and do nothing but watch TV and play video games in my pajamas all day.

Finally, we arrived at Paige's room. I took a deep breath and prepared myself for the worst before we walked in. How sick was she? I trailed behind Kelly as we walked into her room. Her door was closed, but the shade on her window was up.

My aunt opened the door and I peeked around her to assess the situation. I was a little surprised to see Paige sitting up and laughing with Dad, surrounded by a few other Mylar balloons. Mom and Dad must have bought them for her. She also had a bunch of art supplies and games sitting on the table by her bed. It was then that I looked up and realized that I had accidentally grabbed a Batman balloon for my fashionista sister. Oops. While Paige was giving Kelly a hug, I quickly shoved her balloon behind the others. Thankfully, she didn't seem to notice. She flashed me a smile and said "Hey Bryce!"

Paige really didn't look that different than when I saw her before school yesterday. As usual, she had taken the time to style her long hair—this time it was in braids that were looped into two buns on the top of her head. She was wearing her favorite green pajamas with hearts on them. The only thing different about Paige was the small tube coming out of her arm, but she didn't seem too fazed by it. I watched her talking to Kelly and everything seemed weirdly...normal. I hadn't realized how tight my stomach felt until I relaxed a little bit when Dad came over to hug me.

Just then Paige's nurse bounced into her room. She had long, dark hair pulled back in a ponytail, and was wearing a shirt with brightly colored polka dots all over it. As she pressed buttons on a contraption that I now noticed was connected to the tube in Paige's arm, she started to joke around with my sister like they were old friends. As she reached for a blue blood pressure cuff, she and Paige started talking about some singing competition show.

"Did you see the last episode? I can't believe Charlie got voted off! He was amazing. And so cute..." Paige was chatting away, not even bothered by the cuff squeezing her arm. Although, anytime you got my sister started on her favorite shows, a full-on marching band could walk by and she wouldn't notice.

I tried to think of something to add to the conversation, but who was I kidding? I couldn't bring myself to watch five minutes of those reality shows and Paige knew it. And if Paige were seriously sick, why were they sitting there talking about TV? Was I missing something?

I turned around and looked out into the hallway through the window. A little girl who looked a few years younger than Max was walking down the hallway holding her mom's hand. Her mom was pushing a pole behind her that looked just liked Paige's, except hers had a few colorful bags of liquid hanging from the hooks at the top. They both smiled at me as they walked by. I was busy looking at the pole, but when I looked up at the girl's face to smile back, I realized she had no hair. I was relieved they kept walking because I couldn't help but stare at the back of her shiny, bald head.

Paige was going to be devastated if she had to lose her favorite accessory: her hair. Her hair products had practically overtaken all the space in our bathroom. More than once I'd stepped on one of her hair clips in the middle of the night, which is a rude awakening when you're half asleep. What would she do without her hair to put her "bling" in?

Paige's nurse slipped out the door behind me. Dad was talking quietly with Kelly. I tried to talk to Paige normally, even though what I had just seen had left me a bit bewildered.

"So...uh....how are you doing?" I felt weird asking that because she looked fine to me.

"Okay, I guess. Everybody is really nice. I barely slept last night, though. The nurse kept coming in because these pumps kept beeping." Paige pointed to the machines hooked onto the pole by her bed.

I pointed to the tube in her arm. "What do they use that thing for, anyway?"

"It's an IV. They give me water and medicine through it so they don't have to poke me every time. I asked if I could just drink more but the nurse said it was a different kind of water that had to go right into my vein. It was kind of a big needle though. You probably would have fainted if you had to get one!" She laughed and I started to scowl at her, but then I felt bad thinking of her getting this big needle in her arm. She was probably right, anyways. I hated needles.

Dad and Kelly moved out into the hall to talk. Now it was just Paige and me in the room. "Want me to beat you at Uno?" she asked.

"Um, sure. Uh, Paige...what's going on? Are you okay?" I couldn't bring myself to use the "C" word.

Paige's smile faded. "Didn't Aunt Kelly tell you? I have cancer." Her voice got quieter as she said it, and my stomach dropped with a solid *thunk*. We were both quiet for a minute. I really had no clue what to say.

"Are you going to lose your hair?" Stupid, Bryce, stupid. Way to blurt that out.

"Yeah. The medicine I need to get will make my hair fall out. In a few weeks it will probably all be gone." Her voice cracked and her eyes got teary.

"Well, you can wear hats to cover it up." I just wanted to make her feel better, but she glared at me.

"Mom and Dad keep saying it will grow back, and you think it will be fine to just put a hat on? I'm the one who has to walk around bald!"

Oh, geez. I had only been here for ten minutes and already I'd made my sister look like she was going to cry. I thought I should stop talking before I inserted my entire foot into my mouth. I looked down and said, "Paige, this sucks."

She was quiet for a minute and I fiddled with the zipper on my hoodie. "Let's just play Uno," she said softly. I was grateful for a distraction from this conversation.

I sat on the edge of the bed while Paige started to shuffle the cards. "I always forget how big the Uno deck is. It's hard for me to shuffle with my IV in. Can you just do it?" asked Paige. She shoved the deck towards my hands.

As I began to shuffle the deck, I looked out the window of the room and saw Mom and Dad talking to two people who had hospital badges, but were wearing normal clothes. Suddenly Paige interrupted my train of thought.

"That's the child life specialist and the social worker. Kaylee helped me when I got my IV yesterday." Kaylee was a short woman with dark, curly hair. She was standing next to a really big, tall guy who looked like he could play football. "Dion's the social worker. He's been talking to Mom and Dad a lot. They're both really nice."

"So, what do they actually do?" I asked, looking at them skeptically.

"Well, Kaylee mentioned that she does lots of things. She said she helps kids when they are getting pokes, makes sure they understand what's going on with their bodies, and comes up with ways to get through the hard parts of treatment."

"And what about Dion?"

"Mom and Dad said that he's there for them, or me, to talk to if we need support."

Just then, Dad poked his head in. "Bryce, can you come here for a second? There are two people out here Mom and I want you to meet."

I wondered what they wanted to talk to *me* about.

# Chapter 8

# The Talk

Mom gave me a huge hug when I walked out the door. She held me for a minute, her face in my hair, and when she pulled away she wiped a tear from her cheek. Her eyes were red and puffy and it made me sad to look at her, so I turned and looked at Dad. He didn't look much better, but he seemed to be able to talk, at least.

"Bryce, this is Kaylee and Dion. We all just wanted to talk to you for a bit about what's going on with Paige." Kaylee's dimples made her big smile seem extra friendly, and she stuck out her hand to shake mine. I gave her a half-smile and shook her hand.

"Um, sure. I was just about to play Uno with Paige, though."

"That's okay; I'll fill in!" Kelly ducked back into Paige's room. I watched her sit down on the bed next to Paige and start dealing cards.

"There's a room down the hall where we can talk for a few minutes." Dion led the way. "Bryce, part of what Kaylee and I do is work with siblings to help make sure they understand what's going on with their brother or sister, and to help include them in what happens in the hospital. We're also here to answer any questions you have."

"Here we go," I thought to myself. We walked slowly down the hall. I looked down as I walked behind everyone else, hearing the clicks and squeaks of five pairs of shoes on the shiny floor.

As Dion opened the door to the room, I noticed there were way too many chairs squished into the tiny space. It did have a big window that looked out onto a courtyard with trees and a little walking path. The sun was shining, which didn't seem quite right. Given how serious it felt in the room, it seemed like it should be raining outside.

Dion broke the silence. "Bryce, do you know why your sister is in the hospital?" His deep voice and kind brown eyes put me a little more at ease.

"I know she has cancer," I mumbled and looked down. I wasn't sure how much I should say. I peeked at Mom, wishing she would chime in and say, "No she doesn't!" But she just looked sad and her eyes were shiny with tears.

Mom took a deep breath. "You're right, Bryce, Paige does have cancer." When she said *cancer* her voice broke and she looked at Dad. He reached over and took her hand in his.

Dad cleared his throat. He wasn't crying, but his eyes were red. He opened his mouth to talk but it seemed he didn't know what to say. He just looked back at Mom, who was silently crying. I wasn't used to seeing either of my parents get emotional, and my stomach started to flip-flop again.

Kaylee said, "Bryce, I'm sure you have heard of cancer before, but most kids don't know exactly what it is. What do you know about cancer?"

"I mean, I've heard of people having it before, but I guess I don't really know much about it."

"Cancer is when someone has sick cells in their body."

My mind flashed back to the test I'd just taken about cells. I knew that our bodies are made up of billions of cells that all had different jobs. Ms. Reynolds had described them as "building blocks." She hadn't mentioned anything about cells being able to get sick, though, and definitely nothing about cancer.

"So...what happens when your cells get sick? And how does it happen?" I wasn't sure if I was allowed to ask questions yet, but I was curious.

"That's a really good question. When somebody has cancer, it means that one type of cell stops doing its job correctly, and more of these sick cells start to grow really fast, which makes it hard for the healthy cells to do their jobs well. Have you heard of mutations?"

"Sort of..."

"Well, cancer cells are mutated cells. A mutation is a random change in DNA that has the potential to turn everything upside down. So, they have to give Paige medicine and other treatments to get rid of the cancer cells in her body, and to stop any more sick cells from growing and causing problems."

I nodded. That sort of made sense, and the treatment sounded less intimidating when she put it that way.

"There are different types of cancer that kids can have. So each kid gets a specific treatment that is made just for their type. Also, cancer in kids is a lot different than in adults. Even the same type might be treated very differently for a kid than an adult."

"So, how...why...did this happen to Paige?" I asked.

"No one really knows. It is rare, but it sometimes just happens and we don't know why. What we do know is a lot of things that *don't* cause cancer to happen. A lot of siblings are worried that they did something to cause their brother or sister's cancer, or that their brother or sister did something to get cancer, but that is never true. We do know that it is never the fault of the kid who has cancer, and it's not the fault of anybody else. It is an unlucky thing that doesn't happen to many kids, but if it does happen, kids come to a place like this with doctors who know how to fight it."

Unlucky? With all the scientific research out there, that's the best they've come up with?

"Are you okay, honey? Do you have any questions?" Mom was finally able to speak again, although her voice was still shaky.

"Well...how long does Paige have to stay here?"

Mom continued, her voice a little stronger now. "Paige is going to have to be at the hospital for several days to start her medicine, called chemotherapy, or chemo, to make her cancer go away. She'll have to keep coming back every few weeks to get more, but she'll be home a lot in between her treatments, too."

I nodded as Kaylee spoke up again. "Bryce, we just covered a lot of really big stuff with you. Please know that if you have any questions later, Dion and I are always here. We know it's a lot to take in all at once."

Dion added, "You're going through a lot right now. It's totally normal to have all kinds of different feelings about this. But if your feelings become too strong or disruptive; if you are having trouble sleeping, eating, or concentrating at school; or if you would like additional support besides Kaylee and me, it could be helpful to talk to a psychologist or counselor. I can help make that referral should you need one."

Mom kept looking at me like I was suddenly going to fall over. Everyone was watching for my reaction, and I felt my face get hot. I mumbled "okay" to my shoes. What was I supposed to say? I didn't even know what to think.

Dad put his arm around my shoulders. It was quiet in the room, and he whispered, "It's going to be okay, Bryce."

I wasn't sure if he was trying to convince me or himself that this was true. I suddenly felt tired and didn't have the energy to say anything comforting back. This all didn't seem quite real.

"Bryce, your mom and I are going to chat a bit more with Kaylee and Dion. Why don't you head back to Paige's room? We'll head home in a bit." I could tell that they wanted to talk about stuff they didn't want me to hear. This would usually annoy me, but I'd already heard more than I ever wanted to know about cancer.

# Chapter 9
# The Unspoken Question

"Seriously, again?!" I had just lost my fourth Uno game in a row to Paige. And I wasn't even letting her win.

"Ha! I told you, you don't have to take it easy on me just because I'm sick."

"Uh-huh, that's what it is. I just feel bad for you," I replied with a hint of sarcasm, and smiled begrudgingly. Of course I felt bad for Paige, but my competitive side really didn't like to lose.

"Want to watch a movie?" Paige asked, snuggling a little deeper into her bed. I could tell she was getting tired.

"Sure. What do you want to watch?"

"I don't care. There's a stack by the DVD player. Just throw one of those in."

I was going through the stack when Paige's nurse walked in.

"I'm just going to do a quick blood pressure and temperature, okay, Paige?"

"Yeah, that's fine." Paige opened her mouth for the thermometer and held out her arm for the blood pressure cuff. Her nurse wrote down a few numbers and left as I was sliding the DVD into the slot.

"How often do they do that?" I asked, sitting down next to Paige.

"Every four hours or so, even in the middle of the night. It's annoying."

"I'm sure."

About ten minutes into the movie, Mom and Dad walked in.

"Hey, Bryce." Dad was whispering. I looked over and saw Paige was sound asleep.

"I'm going to take you home. I have to get a few things and I may try to take a nap. No one has gotten much sleep, as you can tell." Dad looked over at Paige. "I have a feeling she'll be out for a while anyway."

"Okay." I was a little disappointed. I wanted to stay longer, but I guess there wasn't really any point if Paige was just going to sleep the whole time.

The ride home was really quiet. Dad didn't even turn the radio on. All I heard was the hum of the car as I stared out the window, not really seeing the cars and houses we passed as we drove.

Paige was really sick. "Cancer" was a seriously scary word, and I just couldn't wrap my head around it. The only person I knew who'd had cancer was my Grandpa Jack, and he died from it when I was in first grade.

Was my sister going to die? I didn't dare ask this question out loud. I knew not everybody died from cancer, but obviously, it was a possibility. I felt tears prick my eyes and closed them, willing myself not to cry in front of my dad.

I couldn't imagine our family without Paige. I mean, sure, she drove me crazy sometimes, like all little sisters, but we have always been pretty close overall. I thought back to our last family trip to the beach and how it ended up pouring rain almost the whole time. We were so tired of being cooped up inside, and after two days Paige announced, "Okay, that's it. I have played enough Monopoly to last me a lifetime. Bryce—man up. We are going to the beach!" So we did. We got drenched as we ran around in the sand playing Frisbee; played tic-tac-toe in the wet, compact sand; and finally, since we were already soaked, we just ran right into the ocean for a freezing cold swim. There were times she could be a little dramatic, but her sense of adventure added a lot of fun to our family. I just couldn't imagine life without her.

As we got home and I trudged upstairs, I thought about how scared Paige must be. I couldn't imagine wondering if I was going to die. How could she not be totally freaking out? I flopped onto my bed, still in my clothes. I heard the jingle of Zeke's tags on his collar as he sauntered into my room, and reached down to pull him up with me. I just lay there, with Zeke curled up next to me, his doggy breath in my face. His wrinkled face looked even more sad than usual. I guessed I looked about the same to him.

I pulled out my phone to send Paige a text. I hesitated, not knowing what to say. Finally, I typed: *hey sis- hope ur ok. This really sucks.*

She must have woken up after we left, because a minute later, she responded.

*Thx Bryce. I know. I'll be ok when this is all over.*

I started typing back *promise?* but erased it. There was so much I wanted to say, and ask, but I didn't know where to start. I finally just wrote *U know I luv u. Get better ok?* Then, because I didn't want to be too cheesy, I added *it is much too quiet around here without all ur drama*☺

*Haha. Luv u 2 bro.*

She had to get better. There was just no other option. I closed my eyes and fell asleep, still in my clothes. I woke up a few hours later, disoriented. The clock said that it was seven in the evening. My stomach was growling as I sat up. Zeke gave me a disgruntled look for disturbing his sleep.

I stumbled downstairs, still groggy from my nap. I walked into the living room and saw Dad passed out on the couch. Guess we both needed the sleep. Not wanting to wake him, I headed to the kitchen and poured myself a bowl of cereal, then a second one. It wasn't doing much to fill my hungry stomach, so I looked into the refrigerator to see what else I could find to eat. I grabbed a piece of leftover pizza and ate it cold as I heated up another, and grabbed my backpack.

I needed to at least try to get some homework done before school tomorrow. It was the last thing I wanted to do, but apparently even when your world has flipped upside down, life goes on.

## Chapter 10

# Back to School

The combination of my late nap and thinking about everything going on with Paige made for a long, restless night. I dragged myself into school, yawning, wishing I could just be at home in bed.

"Hey, Bryce, wait up!" Luis ran to catch up with me. "Sorry to hear about your sister. We missed you at practice yesterday. Big game coming up! Are you going to be ready?" I smiled as Luis continued his running commentary the whole way to class, not pausing for me to reply. Typical—that guy could hold a conversation with a statue for twenty minutes before he realized it wasn't talking back. Wait a minute—why did he say he was sorry about Paige? How did he know?

"Bryce! How's Paige?" I heard someone over my shoulder. I turned around to see Jenna, one of Paige's best friends. Her eyes looked huge and she was anxiously twirling a strand of her long, curly hair around her finger, over and over.

"She's okay; obviously not feeling great."

"I can't believe she has cancer."

"I take it she called you, then?"

"I got a text from her last night."

Awesome. Now that Jenna knew, the whole school would know in about two hours. That explains how Luis knew about Paige. Jenna is really nice, but talk about a girl that likes to gossip. Once Jenna gets hold of information, everyone knows.

Between each class, at least one person would stop to ask about Paige. I felt a little thrown off by all the attention and questions. It was probably stupid of me to think I could just slip back into school without anyone knowing. I knew people were just worried about Paige, which was nice, but I was annoyed at having to answer the same questions over and over again. *How's Paige doing? Does she really have cancer? How long will she be in the hospital?*

"Hey, Bryce!" I saw Kelsey coming up behind me. She was the last person I wanted to know about Paige's cancer. I felt like I was finally able to have conversations with her without feeling all flustered. The last thing I needed was her giving me the "pity look" every time she saw me.

"Hey," I said, slowing down so she could catch up. We were in the same Language Arts class so there was no escaping.

"How's your day going?"

"Uh, fine, I guess. You?"

"Pretty good."

It took everything I had not to explode and say, "Actually, my day sucks! No one will leave me alone and I'm sick of everyone asking me about Paige." But I didn't want Kelsey to think I was a horribly selfish person for thinking that. More than anything, though, my day was awful from worrying about my sister and trying to wrap my head around the fact that she was in the hospital, fighting cancer. And there was definitely no way I could go there without totally losing it. I was barely holding it together as it was.

As we sat down in class, I pretended to read my book, hoping that nobody would bother me and ask me more questions. No such luck. Casey, the short stop from our team, sat next to me and pushed his shaggy blonde hair out of his eyes. Before I could turn the subject to our upcoming game, he said, "So, I heard your sister has cancer."

I sighed, gearing up for the same round of Q&A I'd been doing all day. Out of the corner of my eye I saw Kelsey look up from her book. "Uh-huh," I mumbled under my breath, and pretended to be really interested in the chapter I was reading. I hoped he'd get the hint and drop the subject.

"That sucks."

"Yup. It does. But she'll be okay." I didn't take my eyes off the page. I wondered how long it would take for him to realize that I wanted to be left alone.

I somehow forgot that Casey has no filter whatsoever. I was quickly reminded of this, however, when he blurted out, "Is she going to die?" I froze. The words blurred together on the page. Did he really just ask me that?! How was I supposed to answer?

"Casey!" Kelsey blurted out, eyes wide.

"No!" I looked up from my book and glared at him. "Casey, seriously? You just asked if my sister was going to die?"

"I...didn't mean it to come out like that." Casey's cheeks were turning red and he was having a hard time making eye contact with me. "I...I just, I mean, I guess I meant to ask how bad it is? Sorry, if you don't want to talk about it..."

"No, it's okay. She's fine. She'll be fine." I wanted to escape from the room.

"Are you okay?" Kelsey silently mouthed to me, obviously not wanting to create a bigger scene. Her eyes were still wide and even looked a little shiny like she wanted to cry.

"Yeah," I whispered back, then looked away. Great—there was that pity look I didn't want.

Thankfully, Mrs. Rodriguez started talking at that point, and Casey turned around to look at her, his face and neck still bright red. I crossed my arms on the desk and put my head down.

We were definitely on the ride at that point. It felt like we were slowly creeping up the first hill of the coaster, about to pause at the top. You know that feeling when your heart starts to pound because you realize you're about to plunge over the edge? When the anticipation builds as you slowly creep higher and higher and the people on the ground get smaller and smaller? That's exactly how I felt as I sat there, my eyes squeezed shut, trying to block everything out. I knew the plunge was coming; I just didn't know how steep it was going to be or what turn was going to come next.

## Chapter 11

# Talked Out

It was a relief to be back at practice. By the end of the day I had answered so many questions about Paige that I figured there wasn't anyone left to tell about it. Tyson and I started warming up.

"Ready for the game next week?"

"As ready as I can be," I said as I closed my mitt around the ball. I loved the sound of the ball when it hit the glove: *thawp!*

I grabbed the ball out of my mitt to throw back, feeling its familiar weight and the roughness of the seams in my hand.

"Are you?"

"I'm feeling pretty good about it. I think we can beat 'em."

We were quiet for the next few throws.

"So, Paige really has cancer?" Tyson threw the ball. *Thawp!*

Aw, man, seriously? I hadn't gotten to talk to Tyson yet, but I was already so over talking about it. "Yup." *Thawp!*

There was an awkward silence for a few minutes while we threw the ball back and forth. Tyson's never quiet. He was the guy who was always cracking everybody up, the guy who keeps everybody awake talking and laughing until 2 a.m. when we'd spend the night at someone's house. I could tell he was wondering if he should ask more about it or if he should wait for me to say something.

"What was it like?"

"What was what like?" I wasn't sure if we were continuing a conversation, or starting a new one. Did we have to talk about this?

"The hospital. Paige. I mean, is she really sick?"

"The hospital was fine. Kind of creepy, but not as bad as I expected.

Paige is doing okay. She's not feeling great, obviously. Cancer apparently does that to people." There may have been more than a touch of sarcasm in my reply, but I just wanted to focus on baseball. Throw, catch, hit. Simple. Keep my mind off of everything else. Was that too much to ask?

Ty kept the ball in his mitt, tilted his head to the side, and squinted at me. "Ooo-kay, dude, just asking. I mean, this is kind of crazy news."

I rolled my eyes. Why did I feel so angry with Ty? But I couldn't help myself; I was done talking about Paige today. I didn't say anything else. Ty finally threw the ball back to me. It tipped the edge of my mitt and landed on the ground behind me, which made me even more annoyed. I threw the ball back with a little extra pepper on it, and it sailed over Tyson's head.

"Bryce, seriously? What the heck?"

Coach Jacobsen called us in to start some drills, so I just turned and ran in towards the dugout. I saw Jamal looking at me and then looking over at Tyson who had grabbed the ball and was walking more slowly towards Coach.

We were so busy with drills for the rest of practice that I didn't really get a chance to talk to Ty again. When practice ended, I quickly grabbed my stuff and hopped into Dad's car. Kelly was hanging out with Paige at the hospital so my parents could get a little break and have a homemade meal that, as Dad put it, didn't look like plastic hospital food.

"Hey! How was practice? I bet it felt good to finally be back on the field."

"Eh, it was okay." I didn't really feel like getting into it.

"Mom's making your favorite tonight, chili. And some of those biscuits you love."

"Nice. That sounds good. How's Paige today?"

"She's doing a little better than yesterday. I think they found the right combination of medicines to help her not feel so crummy. Hopefully she can come home in a few days. She also got her central line today."

"What's that?"

"It's a little tube that comes out of right here," Dad pointed to his chest as he spoke, "and they can put medicines in it and take blood out of it and stuff. It's kind of cool. Now Paige won't need to get poked all the time." I shuddered at the thought of doctors taking blood out of a tube in my sister's chest.

"Was it good to be back at school?"

"It was fine." It wasn't worth getting in to a big conversation about the eight million questions I had to answer today. Stupid me, thinking that going back to school would take my mind off of what was going on.

It was quiet the rest of the way home. I took off my shoes before I walked in the door and reached down to pet Zeke as his wiggly body greeted me at the door. "Hey, buddy." I bent down so we were nose to nose and scratched him behind his ears. He licked my face and I couldn't help but laugh as I wiped my cheek with my sleeve. Nothing like a little dog slobber to turn your day around.

I could hear Mom setting the table. "Hey, Bryce! Dinner will be ready soon. How was practice?"

"It was fine," I said, dropping my bag by the stairs. "I'm just going to run and take a shower."

I took a fast shower because I knew Mom would have to get back to the hospital right after dinner. As I threw on my sweats I could hear my parents getting into it over something downstairs.

"Sarah, we can't afford that right now. We have to be careful; we're going to have a lot of bills coming up."

"I know it's expensive, Dan, but she'll need it. It will be a great way for her to stay connected to her friends. And that way she won't have to use our laptop all the time."

"It would be nice, but no. We can't get her her own laptop right now. We just can't do it."

I was halfway down the stairs, and although my stomach was rumbling, I stopped and headed back upstairs. I did not want to get in the middle of an argument between my parents. I turned on a video game and tried to distract myself from thoughts of fights, food, and the constant inquisition that was my day today. Dinner could wait, as long as it meant no more talking.

# Chapter 12

# Forgotten

The next day at practice, I was determined to focus on baseball and leave everything else off the field. Even though Tyson and I sat at the same table at lunch, I sat at the end kind of by myself. I didn't feel like having a big conversation with him—or anyone, really—and I guess he didn't want to have one either.

We were all jogging around the bases for our warm-up. I sped up a bit to catch up with Ty and Luis. I didn't want things to be weird with Tyson anymore. "Dude, we have to go see it!" Ty was saying to Luis. "The effects look awesome."

"Effects for what?" I asked.

Luis replied, "That alien movie coming out this weekend."

"Oh, I saw the previews, it does look good!"

Our conversation was cut short by Coach Jacobsen directing us to break up for drills. The infielders had batting practice first, so Ty ran to grab a helmet, while Luis and I headed to the outfield to practice catching fly balls. I heard Tyson call after me, "Better focus out there, Bryce. You still got that case of butterfingers?"

Luis laughed and shoved me lightly on the shoulder as he called back to Tyson, "He'll be fine. I don't see Kelsey on the sidelines to distract him today."

"Ha ha, guys," I said, trying to play it off, but feeling my face get hot. Luckily, I focused all my attention on the ball and had no issues in the outfield. Not that I didn't still get some teasing from the other guys, though.

After practice, I was tossing the ball around, watching as one by one, my teammates left with their parents. 10...15...20 minutes after practice ends, and still no sign of Mom or Dad to pick me and Ty up. I checked my phone a few times to see if they had left a text or a message. Nothing. This was so not like them. I tried calling each of them three times, and each time, the call went straight to voicemail. What was going on?

"Dude, I'll just call my mom. She's probably home by now, anyway. She can just pick us up."

"Let me just try them one more time," I said, pressing "call" yet again.

Finally it started ringing.

"Hi Bryce!" Mom's voice was fuzzy. Wherever she was, the reception wasn't great.

"Mom, where are you?"

"What do you mean where am I? I'm at the hospital. Kelly just got here, so I'm about to head home for a bit to grab some stuff for Paige. How was practice?"

"I'm still here. Where's Dad?"

"He's with you, isn't he?"

"Would I be asking where he is if he was with me?"

Mom's voice got high on the other end of the phone. I couldn't hear everything she was saying, but the gist of it was: they forgot about me! How do your own parents *forget* about you?!

"You know what? Don't worry about it. Ty said his mom is probably home now so she can come get us. I'll be home soon."

"Seriously? Your parents forgot to pick us up?" asked Ty as I hung up the phone.

"Can you believe it? My mom thought my dad was going to get us and my dad probably thought my mom was going to get us."

"And we're the ones who get lectured to be more responsible all the time?"

"Tell me about it." I was glad Ty was making a joke out of it. I, on the other hand, was totally embarrassed. When Ty's mom showed up, she was so nice about having to pick us up, but my face felt hot the whole way home. When the car pulled up to my house, I mumbled "thanks" as I grabbed my stuff and got out.

"Hello?" I yelled as I walked in the door. I wasn't sure if anyone was even home yet.

Mom started walking towards me from the kitchen. "I'm so sorry, honey. Your dad and I got our signals crossed. With Paige still in the hospital we're a little out of it..."

I didn't even bother to respond; I just went up to my room and shut the door. I think Mom could tell how upset I was so she left me alone. Good. I didn't want to talk to her. But after fifteen minutes of sitting up there, feeling embarrassed and mad, it made me even angrier that she didn't come talk to me. She forgot about me and all I got was a lame excuse? I was trying to be understanding about things—I knew how stressed out my parents were. But it wasn't like this week had been easy on me either. When Dad got home, I overheard him talking with Mom while she packed up the last few things to take to the hospital for the night.

"Why is Bryce still upstairs?"

"He's upset because we got mixed up about who was supposed to pick him and Tyson up from baseball today."

"What do you mean we got mixed up? You knew I was working late today—it was your day to pick him up."

"You told me you could leave work early to make it there in time to get them. I had to wait for Kelly to get to the hospital before I could head home!" There was Mom's shrill upset voice again.

"Sarah. I told you I had a meeting, so I couldn't leave work early."

"I can't do this right now, Dan. I have to go."

I heard the front door close and watched out my window as Mom's car pulled away. I rolled my eyes and slumped onto my bed. She didn't even come say goodbye to me. Nice. Forgotten twice in the same day.

# Chapter 13

# Surprise

Even though it had only been a little over a week, it seemed like Paige had been gone for way longer. Strangely, I almost felt like we were getting into a new routine without her at home. I would go to school and practice, Dad would pick me up (apart from the one "incident"), Mom would be home for dinner with us every few nights while Kelly stayed with Paige, and then Mom would drive back to the hospital. Repeat. Repeat. Repeat.

I wished I could have seen Paige more, but it was too difficult for me to get to the hospital on school days. By the time practice was over, it was late and I still had homework. Things were so much quieter around the house now. Honestly, I kinda missed having Paige around. I liked things the way they were before.

I missed having someone to watch Travel Channel shows with. You know those programs where they show the top ten roller coasters in the country, or the most amazing beaches? Paige and I would always scheme about how we were going to talk Mom and Dad into going on a trip to one of those places. Then we would debate which beach looked best or which coaster seemed like the biggest thrill (or the most terrifying, from Paige's perspective).

One time, Mom caught us awake at midnight watching one of those shows. It was all about the Atlantis Resort in the Bahamas, with these amazing water parks and aquariums—we couldn't turn it off. Mom started lecturing us, but Paige and I still couldn't take our eyes off the screen. Then her voice got higher and Paige said, "But Mom, look at this place!" When Mom turned to the TV her eyes got huge and she asked, "Where is that?!" and sat down in between us to watch the rest. By the end of it, all three of us were trying to figure out how to convince Dad to take us there, and we didn't get to sleep until 1:00 in the morning.

Dinners were so quiet without the whole family around. I actually missed Paige giggling about silly gossip from school. Usually we all ate together in the dining room, but it didn't feel quite right with just two of us at the table, so we had been eating in front of the TV. And lately, it was either a quick microwave dinner, or yet another casserole from a neighbor. It was nice of people to bring food, but after the fourth lasagna in a week I was craving some of my dad's famous pulled pork sandwiches, or my mom's pumpkin waffles she sometimes made for our ritual of breakfast for dinner on Wednesdays. Even Zeke was thrown off by the change in the family routine. Sometimes at night I would find him sleeping in front of Paige's door.

We were definitely ready for Paige to come home and for all of us to be under one roof again.

"I'm going to change before dinner," I said, as I opened the front door after a long, hard practice that had ended in the rain.

"Hey, before you do that, there's something for you in the living room. You should go check it out."

"For me?" We'd had what seemed like a million packages delivered recently, but they had all been for Paige. I wondered who would have gotten me something.

I turned the corner into the living room to see Paige watching TV on the couch.

"Bryce!"

"Hey!" I ran over to give her a hug. I couldn't remember the last time I had hugged my sister. I was just so happy to see her.

"Why didn't you tell me you were coming home today?"

Mom chimed in, "Plans change so quickly at the hospital. We didn't want to get your hopes up and then have it fall through."

"Yeah, and I wanted to surprise you!" Paige said with a beaming smile on her face.

"Well, it worked. I had no idea!"

"It's good to see you! But, Bryce...you kinda stink," said Paige, wrinkling up her nose.

"I know, I know. It was a rough practice today."

"Why don't you get cleaned up, honey, and then we'll have dinner?" My mom opened up a box and I smelled a delicious waft of Kung Pao chicken. They must have picked up Chinese food on their way home—yum. Even though it wasn't home cooking, a feast of Chinese takeout would hit the spot after running around in the mud all afternoon.

Who would have guessed that a simple dinner as a family of four would be so exciting?

## Chapter 14

# Doughnuts and Rainbows

That Saturday morning, Kelly and Max came over to visit. Kelly walked in the door with a box of doughnuts in one hand and a brown paper bag in the other. I was too busy grabbing a maple bar to think about what might be in the other bag. Mmmm...it was still warm.

"There aren't any more maple bars?" Paige asked, looking in the box.

"No, there was only one left at the store. There's a chocolate one with cream in the middle, though—you love those," Kelly said, setting her purse down on the counter.

"Well, but...Bryce's maple bar looks really good," Paige said, staring at me.

I felt everyone's eyes on me as I was about to take a bite.

"What?" I asked, looking around.

"Bryce, would you mind trading with Paige? She really hasn't eaten a lot these past few days and the fact that anything looks good to her is kind of a big deal." Mom was holding the chocolate doughnut out to me.

Seriously? I never got doughnuts and maple bars were my favorite kind. However, at this point, with everyone staring at me, it really didn't seem like I had a choice in the matter.

"All right, fine. Here you go, Paige." I handed the maple bar to her.

"Thanks, Bryce!" Paige grabbed the maple bar and took a bite as Kelly reached into the other bag.

"Ta-da!" With a flourish, Kelly pulled out a couple bottles of hair dye. Paige's eyes lit up. After that big deal about switching doughnuts, Paige clearly had already forgotten all about her maple bar. She tossed it on a plate and grabbed one of the bottles. I quickly snagged a bite of the forgotten confection and wondered what all the excitement was about.

"Well, Paige, if you're going to lose your hair you might as well let it go out in style!"

I dug into my doughnut as I looked at all the colors Kelly had brought: pink, purple, green, blue. Then I looked at Mom out of the corner of my eye. I figured she would be freaking out, but she had a sparkle in her eye.

"Can I, Mom?"

Mom nodded. Paige squealed, grabbed Kelly's hand, and dragged her upstairs. I turned my attention back to the chocolate frosting on my fingers.

Dad was next to me, eating a jelly doughnut and reading the front page of the paper. With a rustle, he took out the sports section and handed it to me so I could get the scoop about spring training. When Mom reached into the box and grabbed an apple fritter, I must have looked surprised, because she grinned sheepishly and said, "Hey, it's a celebratory weekend, right?"

Max spent most of the morning showing me the superhero action figures he brought with him, flying them around in circles and tormenting poor Zeke. I was contemplating whether Paige would notice if I finished her abandoned maple bar when my aunt bounded downstairs.

"And now, on the red carpet, may I present..." Kelly looked at me pointedly. I started thumping my hands on the table for the drum roll and Kelly dramatically pointed her arms up the stairs as she continued, "...the new Paige!"

My parents clapped as Paige strutted down the stairs, pretending to be a model. I couldn't help myself—I burst out laughing. Her hair was a rainbow! Paige had a huge smile on her face and she did a twirl. I glanced at Mom and saw her eyes well up with tears. Of course, Dad had to get out the camera to take some pictures.

"Awesome! Mom, can I dye my hair?" asked Max.

"Sorry, little dude," said Kelly, smiling. "The medicine that Paige has to take is going to make her hair fall out, so this rainbow look is only temporary."

"Aw, man. I never get to do anything fun!" Never one to stay focused on anything for too long, Max made Batman jump off the back of the chair, then fly into the other room to crash the Lego tower he'd built earlier.

"Wow, Paige. I've never seen anything quite like that before!"

"I know, it's a little crazy. But hey, if it's going to fall out, it may as well go out with a bang. Besides, when again in my life is Mom going to let me have rainbow hair?"

"Good point," I said.

"Paige, I'll shave my head when your hair falls out," said Dad, putting his arm around Paige.

"I will too, Paige!" I blurted out, then instantly regretted making the offer without thinking it through. Dad gave me a big proud smile. My regret turned quickly to guilt, for questioning it. Paige didn't have a choice about being bald, and she actually cared what her hair looked like. I should just man up and shave my head—I could always wear a hat. But what if people looked at me funny? My guilt grew even deeper as I realized what I was really thinking—what would Kelsey think if she saw me bald?

My thoughts were interrupted by Paige striking model poses in the mirror with Kelly, then busting out laughing. "Mom, can you take a picture of me with my phone? I want to text it to Jenna. She's going to freak out!"

"Sure, honey. One, two, three, smile!" Mom snapped a picture as Paige pointed to her hair with a huge grin.

## Chapter 15

# Left Out

Sunday was an all-around dreary day. Dad was reading the paper with Zeke curled up at his feet. Even Zeke didn't want to go outside because it was so wet.

"What are you going to do today, honey?" Mom asked as she walked in, carrying two new bottles of hand sanitizer. Dad joked that we should buy stock in hand sanitizer. Mom was completely paranoid about Paige getting exposed to germs. I had been told several times in the past few days how serious it was for a cancer patient to get sick. *Not because of the cancer itself. Because of the treatment. It zaps her immune system for a while so she is more prone to infections.* I wouldn't be surprised if Paige's friends had to fill out a medical history form before they could come visit her, to make sure they weren't bringing in germs to pass on.

"I don't know yet. I have a little homework left, but I got most of it done yesterday."

"Why don't you go see a movie or something? I'd be happy to drive you."

I remembered talking to Ty and Luis about that alien movie the other day. I didn't really feel like doing much, but figured I may as well see what other people were up to. I pulled out my phone to text Tyson.

*Want 2 go see alien movie 2day?*

A few minutes went by. *Saw it yesterday. It was awesome.*

Wait, seriously? Nice of them to invite me!

Then, another text. *Knew Paige was home, figured u were having family time or would have asked u to come.*

They still could have asked me. That was not cool. I tossed my phone to the side.

"What time do you want me to drop you off?" Mom asked.

"I don't really feel like going out. I think I'm just going to hang around here."

"You sure? Paige will probably just sleep most of the day and your dad is on the hook to clean out the garage."

"Yeah, it's fine. I'm going to go upstairs for a bit."

"You okay?"

"Yeah, fine. Just a little tired."

I tossed my phone onto my bed just as it chimed that a text had come through. It was Tyson again.

*Want 2 go 2 the mall?*

So *now* he wants to hang out? I wanted to get out of the house, but I didn't want Tyson to hang out with me just because he felt bad. I would rather just be by myself.

*Just gonna hang here,* I responded.

I put my phone on the dresser as it chimed again, but didn't bother to look at it this time. As I listened to the rain pouring down in sheets, I grabbed the book off my nightstand, plopped myself onto my bed, and opened to the next chapter, hoping to tune out the world for a little while.

# Chapter 16

# The Fruity-O Debacle

"Bryce! I told you not to touch my stuff!" Paige yelled from her room.

"What are you talking about?" I asked, walking to her doorway.

"My phone! I can't find it! Where did you put it?" Paige was tossing things aside, barely even looking under them before she tossed the next thing over. "I told you not to touch my stuff!" she yelled again, tears starting to stream down her puffy cheeks. Wow, she really had changed in just a few weeks. My parents had warned me that one of the medications she was taking would make her cranky and give her "moon face," and make her crazy hungry sometimes. They told me it was a steroid, but not like the kind you hear athletes getting in trouble for taking. The steroid she had to take was part of her chemo.

"What are you talking about? I didn't touch your phone."

"Well, someone did, and now I can't find it! Just get out!"

I turned around just in time to see Mom coming to intervene.

"It's probably best just to walk away," Mom whispered to me as she walked into Paige's room. I didn't argue, quietly turning and heading back down the hall.

"Here it is, honey!" I heard Mom say as she lifted up a pile of clothes from Paige's desk chair.

Paige hadn't exactly been a peach to be around the past week. I tried to be patient because I knew it was the meds that made her act that way, but I only had so much patience. If I treated Paige the way she had been treating me recently, I would have been grounded for a month.

Sitting down at the table, I was about to pour the milk into my cereal when I heard Paige open and close the cabinets.

"Are we out of Fruity-O's?"

"I finished them yesterday. Mom said she would buy more when she goes to the store today."

"Bryce! That is the only thing I can eat right now! Everything else tastes like cardboard! Why did you finish them?"

I didn't answer and went back to eating my cereal.

"Bryce, seriously, I am starving all the time, all I want to eat is Fruity-O's, and you just eat them without considering anyone else?" Paige apparently was not going to let this go.

I wasn't going to say anything, knowing that she'd probably start crying no matter what I said. But then, as I was about to take a bite, I found a piece of green hair floating in my cereal. I lost it.

"Paige! I ate them because they sounded good and I didn't see your name written on the box! And now I can't eat this bowl of cereal because your hair is in it! Can't you just shave it off already? It's everywhere!"

I made a big display of having to dump out my cereal, pour myself a new bowl, and put my non-spoon-holding hand up to block any incoming hairs from my breakfast.

Paige just looked at me, with her patchy rainbow-colored hair and tears streaming down her face. I knew it was a low blow, but a guy can only take so much. Her hair had been falling out like crazy all week. Now she actually *looked* like she had cancer.

"I'm sorry, Paige," I said, putting down my spoon. Paige just sat there crying. "I'm sorry," I said again.

Once again, Mom came to the rescue. She walked over, putting her arm around Paige.

"It's okay, honey. It's okay."

Paige stopped crying and glared at me with the new, evil look she had acquired. Ever since starting her medicine, she had been an emotional wreck. I took one last bite of my cereal and went to grab my backpack.

That day at school, I went through the motions of my morning, and barely heard what the teachers were saying.

"Dude, you okay?" Tyson asked as he sat down next to me at lunch.

"Yeah, why?"

"You just look at little out of it."

"I'm fine," I said flatly, taking my sandwich out of my bag.

"How's Paige these days?"

"She's okay. Her hair is starting to fall out and she's been super grumpy recently."

"That sucks."

"What sucks?" asked Luis as he slid into the chair across from me.

"Paige," replied Tyson.

"Paige doesn't suck. Her grumpiness does," I corrected him.

"Ooh, moody girls. Welcome to my life." Luis had two older sisters. "Hey. Do you guys have anything going on this weekend? Do you want to go bowling tomorrow afternoon?"

"I'm in," said Tyson.

"Me, too," I chimed in. Ever since Paige's diagnosis, I had barely gotten to hang out with Tyson and Luis outside of school. I was more than happy to escape the drama at my house.

# Chapter 17

# Connect

"Honey, we should probably be ready to go by about two o'clock," Mom said as I was eating my cereal the next morning (not the Fruity-O's, though. I wouldn't dare eat those again anytime soon).

"Go where? I'm going bowling with Ty and Luis."

"That sibling support group I told you about. I think it's called 'Connect' or something. I told you about it last week."

"That's today? Mom, I already told them I could go bowling today."

"Honey, this is important. You can go bowling with them anytime. This group only meets once a month, and I really want you to go. Just ask the guys if you can go tomorrow instead."

"They can't go tomorrow. Tyson has his grandma's birthday party."

"Well, I'm sorry, but I really want you to go to the support group today. I think it will be good for you to meet some kids that are going through the same things you are."

Great. I had finally planned something with my friends for the first time in weeks and now I had to bail. I figured they would never invite me to do anything again.

"What is this support group thing again?"

"It's a group at the hospital for kids who have a brother or sister who is sick. Dion said kids really like it. You don't have to talk if you don't want to, but I at least want you to listen."

I pictured a bunch of sad-looking kids sitting in a circle being forced to talk about their feelings. It didn't sound like a ton of fun to me.

I pulled my phone out to text Tyson. *My mom signed me up for some hospital group thing. can't go bowling.*

*That stinks. I'll hit an extra strike for u.*

I was hoping he would say we could all go bowling next weekend, but I guess I couldn't expect them to reschedule just because I couldn't go. This was so not fair.

I kept my headphones in as we drove to the hospital, since I was annoyed and didn't want to talk. Mom parked so she could go in with me. When we walked in, a few minutes late, it looked like the kids were in the middle of playing a game. It was loud and everybody was talking and laughing— were we in the right place? This did not look like a therapy group, or at least not what I expected one to look like.

A guy who looked college-age came over to me. He had longish brown hair that he kept brushing away from his eyes.

"Hey there! You must be new to our group this month. I'm Kevin."

"I'm Bryce." I didn't really know what else to say. I was still taking in the chaos.

"Hey, Bryce! Come join us if you want. We're playing 'Human Bingo.'"

Mom looked beyond excited as she waved and walked out the door. I rolled my eyes a little, but trailed after Kevin as he explained the game.

"Your card has a bunch of facts on it. You're supposed to go around the room asking people if they have these things. If you do, you put an 'X' on that square. The first person to fill their card wins. It's a fun way to get to know each other. Like this." He pointed to a square on his board that said *Has a dog.* "Do you have a dog?"

"I do."

"See, now I get to X off that box, and I just learned something about you."

I took the bingo card and stood in the middle of the room, feeling a little lost.

A girl with a long, black ponytail swinging behind her walked up to me and introduced herself.

"I'm Cat. You must be the new guy."

"That's me. I'm Bryce."

"Let's see...what do I have left? Have you been to Disneyland?"

"I have. Hold on; I need to get some of mine marked off. Do you have a cat?"

"Nope, sorry. But my favorite sport is soccer, so you can mark that one off."

"Cool, thanks."

"My brother has a brain tumor. He's had it for a while, so I've been coming here for like a year. What brings you here?"

"My younger sister has cancer."

She sure was chatty. She went on and on about all the stuff they'd done throughout the past year.

I heard Kevin's voice from across the room. "All right; it looks like we have a winner! Everyone take a seat." Kevin was letting the winner pick a piece of candy from a big orange bowl.

"We have some new people joining us this month. Let's go around and introduce ourselves. Go ahead and say your name, your brother or sister's name, what they have, and the worst thing about them being sick. Bryce, why don't you start us off?"

Oh, geez. I wasn't the biggest fan of speaking in front of a bunch of strangers.

"Uh, okay. My name is Bryce. My little sister Paige has cancer and the worst part of her being sick is..." I paused here. I had never really thought about what the worst thing was—it all kind of sucked. "Um, I guess maybe missing out on doing some things with my friends." I just kind of blurted it out.

"Yeah, it's hard when you feel that disconnect. Well, we're happy to have you join us, Bryce. Cat, why don't you go next?"

"Hey, I'm Cat. My brother has a brain tumor, and I'm going to have to go with Bryce on this. The worst part of him being sick is missing out on time with my friends. I couldn't meet my friends at the mall last week because my brother had to go to the emergency room, and I was not happy. I'm getting a little sick of it."

"It sounds like this is a common theme. Anyone else feel like they are missing out on stuff?"

Almost everyone's hand went up.

"I missed a huge party a few weeks ago because we were out of town visiting the place where my sister is going to get her bone marrow transplant."

"I missed my track meet last weekend because my brother had to get blood at the hospital and it took forever. And it's not like my parents would have had to time to watch it anyway. Every day someone different drives me home from practice."

"Me, too!" I blurted out. "A few weeks ago my parents forgot to pick me up at all!" I said, surprised to find myself laughing as I told the story.

"Now that's pretty bad," said a boy whose nametag said *Chris*.

"Great, thanks for the discussion, everyone. Let's finish introducing ourselves and then we're going to do an activity around this."

When the last person had introduced himself, Kevin started handing out pieces of paper and markers.

"Okay. I want each of you to write down words that describe what it's like to have a brother or sister who is sick. I want this to be stream of consciousness, so you have five minutes to write down as many words as you can."

I stared at my blank sheet and started writing. By the time the five minutes were up my page was almost filled with words like *sad, frustrating, confusing,* and *lonely.*

"Okay, does anyone want to share a few words they put down?"

"Annoying."

"Scary."

"Frustrating."

I had a couple of those words on my list, too.

"Okay, these are great. I'm going to give you another five minutes and on the other side of your paper I want you to write words that describe how you deal when you're feeling these words you just shared."

I flipped my page over and thought for a minute before I started writing: *baseball, reading, music.* I kept thinking and adding to my list until Kevin called "Time!"

"Okay. I'm going to collect these. Sarai is going to lead you guys in a game of Pictionary while I work on some stuff with your lists."

We broke into teams while Kevin sat at a computer in the corner typing stuff from our lists.

The rest of the hour went by quickly as we played Pictionary. I was not the best artist by far, but nobody took the game too seriously. By the end, Chris and I were laughing hysterically at a drawing I tried to do of a moose, and we didn't care that much that we got beaten by the other team.

"Okay, guys, let's wrap up!" Kevin started to hand out pieces of paper. "These are called word clouds. The first page shows the words you guys used to describe what it's like to have a brother or sister who is sick. The second page shows the words you used to describe how you deal. You can do whatever you want with these. You can show them to your parents or friends so they can get a glimpse into what life is like for you, or you can keep them to yourselves so when you're feeling upset, you can remind yourself how to deal."

Kevin walked by, handing me my papers. The words I had written down earlier were printed in all different colors and fonts, some of them big, some small. It looked really cool.

"Great job today, guys. We'll see you next month! Remember, if anything comes up between now and then, feel free to email me."

"Well, what did you think?" Chris asked as he grabbed his backpack.

"It was pretty fun. Better than I expected."

He laughed and said, "Yeah, I was so annoyed when my mom signed me up a few months ago, but it is kinda fun. See you next month, then?"

"Definitely. If you want to hang out before then just text me." We quickly exchanged numbers.

"Will do. See ya!"

"Later."

I looked up just in time to see Mom waving excitedly from across the room. She could be so embarrassing sometimes.

"How was it?"

"Pretty fun, actually."

"I'm so glad! What's that?" she asked, pointing to my papers.

"Oh nothing, just an activity we did." I felt better just keeping those to myself for the time being.

# Chapter 18

# Enlisted

That Monday after school, I tried to explain "Human Bingo" to Tyson as his mom drove us home from practice.

"It was kind of a cool way to get to know random facts about people."

Tyson looked at me skeptically. "Dude, did they take over your brain or something? How did you have so much fun at a therapy session?"

I laughed a little, although his sarcasm stung me a bit. "I was worried about going, but it wasn't all touchy-feely like I thought it was going to be."

"I don't know. It still sounds a little weird."

"Well, I guess you had to be there." I couldn't put my finger on it, but it was starting to feel like unless someone lived this, they just couldn't really get it. It was like trying to describe the g-force you felt on the Screamroller. You had to feel it to get it. Everything that came along with cancer seemed to push me and Ty apart a little more. I wished he could try to understand where I was coming from.

Tyson's mom pulled into our driveway. I grabbed my backpack and opened the door.

"Thanks, Mrs. D. See ya, Tyson."

"See ya tomorrow."

When I got home, the house was empty. Where was everyone? It was kind of nice having the place to myself, though. Paige seemed to be the ruler of the remote lately—I had watched enough girlie Disney shows to last me a lifetime.

Zeke snuggled on the couch next to me. Mom never let him on the couch when she was home, but I bet he probably felt pretty neglected lately, too. Nobody was paying much attention to either of us these days.

"Zeke, let's watch a manly show, just us boys." He responded by setting his head on my lap and I rubbed his ears as we both relaxed. I had barely started a second episode of *Dirty Jobs* when I heard the garage door open and close, and then Paige slumped on the couch next to me. She grabbed the remote and changed the channel.

"Hey! I was watching that!"

I looked over at her. She didn't even seem to be looking at the TV. She was just staring at the painting of the beach we bought on our trip to Mexico last spring.

"You okay?"

"I don't know. I guess I should be happy but...Dr. Z said I can go back to school next week."

"That's good, right? You keep complaining about missing out on what your friends are doing."

"I know, but what will the kids say when they see how different I look?"

I guess I was used to how Paige looked now, but it was true: she did look different. She was completely bald now, and she still had puffy cheeks from her steroids.

"I talked to Kaylee in clinic about going back to school, and she said that she could visit my class before I have to go back for the first time. They'll make sure the kids understand about my cancer and then people can ask questions and stuff."

"That sounds like a pretty good idea." Zeke looked up at me as if to say, *that quiet guy time didn't last too long.*

"Kaylee also mentioned that maybe you can go with them...to talk to my class? Since they know you and all..." She trailed off, looking down at her fingers.

I was surprised, but I kind of liked the idea. I knew more than I had ever wanted to know about cancer. And maybe if Paige actually came back to school, people would stop asking me all the time how she was doing.

"Yeah, I can do that."

"Thanks, Bryce." Paige looked at me with a half-smile. She looked a little relieved. "Mom said she'll figure out a time to bring you in to meet with Kaylee to talk about what you'll say."

Good thing I said yes. It sure sounded like they were already planning on it.

# Chapter 19

# Teacher Bryce

I got to miss math class to do the presentation on Friday. After Paige's teacher quieted the class, Kaylee started the talk.

"Hi! My name is Kaylee. I work at the hospital where Paige is getting her treatment. And I'm assuming that a lot of you already know Bryce," she said, pointing in my direction. "Most of you know that Paige has cancer. Have any of you known somebody else who has had cancer?" A lot of people raised their hands, and a couple of kids started talking at once, shouting out that their uncle or grandma had cancer.

"It looks like most of you know somebody who has had cancer. Bryce and I are going to talk to you today about what cancer is, and how we treat it to try to make it go away."

"I know you all have learned what cells are, but do you know that cells are what make up everything in our body? Every cell has its own job, to make your body run right. Sometimes, some cells stop doing their job correctly. Usually, your body realizes this and stops these cells from growing. But sometimes, these sick cells keep growing and replicating really quickly. These are cancer cells. These may be cells that grow in a person's blood, like with leukemia. Or the cells may clump together and form a tumor somewhere in a person's body."

Now it was my turn to chime in. I felt a little nervous as I started out. My heart was pounding like it always does when I have to make a presentation.

"If somebody has cancer cells in their body, they need to get treatment to fight and get rid of these cells, and make sure no new sick cells keep growing. So the doctors give medicine called chemotherapy, or use an x-ray treatment called radiation, or sometimes even both. Paige has already started chemo and will later have radiation to treat her cancer."

A boy sitting towards the back of the room yelled out, "Radiation? Isn't that what turned the Hulk into a superhero?" A bunch of kids laughed. I wasn't sure how to respond.

Kaylee interjected with a smile, "That is how the story goes, but this radiation only helps zap those cancer cells. However, I think Paige must have super strength because she sure is fighting this cancer like a hero!"

I bit back a laugh. That was a little cheesy. Besides, I had the thought that it wasn't the radiation but those nasty steroids that seemed to turn Paige into the angry Hulk.

Kaylee brought along a central line so the kids could see that Paige didn't have to get shots all the time. She also had Paige's teacher put out a question box before our visit so that kids could put questions in there that they were too embarrassed to ask. Kaylee started reading some of them.

"Is it true Paige has no hair? Will it grow back?"

Kaylee answered, "Yes, Paige has lost her hair and is bald, but it will grow back once she finishes her treatment. She may look a little different, but the most important thing to remember is that she is still Paige."

"How did Paige catch cancer?"

I answered this one, making sure to be really clear that it is *impossible* to catch cancer. I didn't want them to be afraid to be around my sister when she came back, or to act grossed out around her or anything. "It's not like a cold that you can pass on to someone else."

Kaylee spoke up, "Right. But along those lines, because Paige's body is working so hard to fight the cancer cells, it's really important for her to avoid catching anything from someone else. If there is anything going around the school, Paige might have to stay home to try to avoid the germs. It's really important for all of you to be really careful to keep your hands washed with soap and water or hand sanitizer."

Then came *the* question from the question box.

"Is Paige going to die?"

I still didn't understand how someone could just ask that big, scary question. I guess I felt like if I didn't say it out loud, then it couldn't happen. I thought back to when Casey had asked me that same question. I looked at Kaylee to see how she was going to field this one. I certainly didn't want to be the one who had to answer that in front of all these kids.

Kaylee said, "This is the scariest question of all, isn't it? All of Paige's doctors and nurses are specialists, which means the only thing they do is help kids with cancer. Everyone is working really hard to try to make sure that Paige gets better."

I wished that she had just said *no, she's not going to die.*

The rest of the presentation went pretty well. Kaylee brought some cool stuff for the kids to see and they got really into checking out the "doctor" stuff. I needed to head back to class soon. I thought about giving the kids in her class a warning that nobody better make fun of my little sister. I looked at that squirrelly kid who'd asked about the radiation and wondered if he would make a stupid comment to Paige or ask her weird questions.

Paige's teacher, Mrs. Edwards, stood up and said, "Bryce, please tell Paige how excited we all are to have her back in class again. Everyone, please give a round of applause to thank our special guests today for coming to talk with us." As I walked out, I thought Paige would do just fine, but I also knew I'd be swinging by to check on her, at least her first day back, just to make sure she was doing okay.

# Chapter 20

# Paige's First Day

As Monday morning rolled around, I could tell Paige was anxious. Before we left for school, she took even longer than usual to get ready. I imagined she was a little nervous about seeing everyone for the first time. When I finally had my turn in the bathroom to brush my teeth, there were four different outfits strewn across the room. Mom was in Paige's room helping her choose the scarf that coordinated best with her outfit, to tie around her head.

"Ugh, my stupid cheeks!" Paige groaned, looking in the mirror. She pushed her hands against her puffy face.

"You look fine, Paige," I said, giving her what I thought was an encouraging smile in the mirror.

"Fine? That's it?" Paige said, stomping back into her room to go through her closet again.

Seriously. I could never win.

We pulled up to the school and Mom parked so she could go in with Paige and talk to the school nurse. Mom got out of the car, but Paige just sat there, fiddling with the buckle on her backpack.

"Um...Paige? You okay?"

She clicked and unclicked the buckle, and didn't say anything. Then, finally, she said, "I'm not so sure about this. Maybe I should wait a few more weeks before I come back to school."

"Paige, your friends are all so excited to have you back in class. You'll probably feel like a celebrity with all the attention you'll get." I could only imagine how weird it must have felt, coming back to school after so long, especially coming back bald.

"This boy in your class asked if when you get radiation, you get special powers like a superhero!" I didn't tell her which superhero—maybe she would think it was Superwoman rather than the angry green one.

She gave me a lopsided smile, with one squinty eye, the one she gets when she tries not to laugh. "I can guess who made that comment." Her smile faded. "Do you think kids will make fun of me?"

"Some kids will probably say dumb things, but I think it helped that we talked with them on Friday. When I first came back to school, kids asked me tons of questions about you, but then they moved on. In your class, they already know all the answers. You are pretty lucky to have such an awesome big brother to explain things to them!" I grinned at her. "Just stick with your friends and you'll be fine. But if anybody does say something, go with the superhero thing, and pretend you have some crazy power so they'll be afraid to mess with you."

I got the half-smile from her again. Taking a deep breath, Paige opened the door. I grabbed her shoulder and she turned to look at me.

"It'll be okay, Paige. And if it's not, you come find me. I have a few superpowers too, you know. It comes along with being a big brother." I gave her a big, theatrical wink along with this statement, and my cheesiness seemed to cheer her up a bit. She rolled her eyes, but her smile was bigger. She took a deep breath and got out of the car.

"Thank you," Mom mouthed to me as we got out of the car.

As we walked into school, Mom walked towards the nurse's office and I gave Paige a nudge. "You'll be fine, okay?"

"I guess..."

"PAIGE!" Jenna shrieked, running up to her and linking her arm through Paige's.

"Hey." Paige gave Jenna an apprehensive smile.

"I am SO glad you are back. Let's get to class!"

"I just have to wait for my mom. She went to talk to the nurse."

"Okay. I'm going to run so I'm not late. I'm so glad you're back!" Jenna shrieked again as she hugged her one more time. All that shrieking! I shook my head, but Paige looked a lot more relieved as Mom came out of the nurse's office.

"Do you want me to walk you to class?" Mom asked.

"Nah, I think I'll be okay. I just ran into Jenna and she's there already, so I'll be fine."

"Okay. Well, if you get too tired, just go see the nurse and she'll call me to come pick you up."

"Sounds good. Bye, Mom."

"Have a good day, honey," Mom said, giving Paige a hug.

"Bye, Mom!" I yelled as she started to walk away.

"Oh, gosh! Bye, Bryce!" She hurried back to give me a hug. Figured.

Throughout the day I went out of my way to run into Paige a few times in the hallway, just to check on her. It looked like she was happy to be back. Whenever I saw her, she was with her usual group of friends, giggling about something. When the last bell rang I made my way over to the sixth grade lockers and walked up behind Paige.

"Well, was it as bad as you thought it would be?" I asked.

"Not at all. I think you talking to everyone before I came back really helped."

"Of course it did. I was pretty awesome."

"Well, thank you for your awesomeness," Paige said, smiling as she rolled her eyes at me.

"I have to get to practice. I just wanted to check in. I'll see you at home." I was actually impressed that Paige made it through the whole day. I probably would have cut out of there early if I knew I had the option.

"Sounds good. See ya. And thank you again, Bryce."

"No problem." I turned to leave with a smile on my face, feeling good about helping her out.

# Chapter 21

# Fan-less

On Friday night, Luis and I were warming up before the game, throwing each other pop flies in the outfield.

"All right, guys, let's bring it in!" Coach yelled from the dugout.

As Luis and I ran towards the infield, my eyes flashed over to the bleachers where the fans sat. Kelsey was there with Becca. As I scanned the other faces, I didn't see any of my family there.

I felt my frustration mounting as I walked into the dugout and slumped on the bench. I tuned out my coach's pep talk as I stared at my mitt, wondering why they were missing the game this time. Before Paige got cancer, at least one of my parents was there rooting me on at pretty much every game. Since she was diagnosed, Dad had been to only one game.

Tyson nudged me and I raised my eyes to look up. Everyone was standing in a circle with their hands stretched out toward the center, and Coach was looking expectantly at me. I jumped up, put my hand on top of the pile, and tried to put my energy into yelling "Go Tigers!" with my teammates before we left the dugout to take our places on the field.

Coach grabbed me by the bill of my hat on my way out and looked me in the eyes. "Bryce...head in the game, okay?"

I looked away and mumbled, "Sorry, Coach."

His hand went from my hat to my shoulder and squeezed. "You okay?"

I took a breath. "I'm good."

"All right, go get 'em!" he said, back with his usual gruff coach voice.

I ran out to left field and tried my best to focus on the game. I found myself looking over at the stands every so often, wondering if at least Dad would show up late to watch me play. Good thing nobody hit the ball my way that first inning.

Second inning, I was on deck, swinging the bat to warm up, and I looked over at the bleachers again. Nope. I gave up; obviously nobody was coming. This was one of those times I felt like I was on the loop of our roller coaster ride with cancer. It was like life was flipped upside down and backwards, and I couldn't do anything about it.

My anger started rising up and I swung the bat even harder as I waited for my turn. Jamal hit a single and I stepped up to the plate.

I took a breath and narrowed my eyes as I looked at the pitcher. He wound up and threw the ball hard. I swung...and missed. I felt the heat in my face reach my stomach as my anger simmered even more. Again, I faced the pitcher, waited for the windup, kept my eyes glued to the ball as it came closer. I swung and smacked the ball with every ounce of energy I had. I heard the loud crack as it connected and the ball started flying towards center field. I ran as hard as I could towards first. As I rounded toward second I saw the third base coach waving to me frantically to keep going. My legs were moving as fast as I could make them run, towards third and then—the third base coach waving and calling out "Go, go, go, Bryce!"—I sprinted towards home. I slid into the base seconds before the ball landed in the catcher's mitt.

Jamal had been jumping up and down at home after scoring his run, and he dived on top of me hollering "Home run!!!!" I was out of breath but laughing as we both got up. I dusted off my pants and felt Tyson careen into me and lift me a foot off the ground. He spun in a circle shouting "Woo-hoo!" and placed me back down again. I ran into the dugout and high-fived my teammates.

My first home run! Man, did that feel amazing. I sat down with a grin and Coach patted me on the back as he walked back out of the dugout. We all quieted down a bit as Casey stepped up to bat, and focused on the game.

After we sealed our victory and congratulated the other team on a well-fought match, we grabbed our stuff and headed off the field.

Kelsey gave me a huge hug. "A home run, Bryce! So awesome!" I could feel my face getting warm again, this time from a mix of pride and embarrassment.

Then I saw Mom's car pulling into the lot next to the field and immediately my mood shifted. Oh, really, *now* they show up? As she got out of the car and started running over towards us I felt Tyson nudge me as he teased, "Aw, your mom's gonna be so proud of her little boy's home run..."

"Don't mention it to her," I snapped. I quickly muttered goodbye to Kelsey and started walking towards Mom.

"What's up with him?" I heard Ty asking Kelsey under his breath. He sounded annoyed, but I didn't really care.

"Bryce!" she said breathlessly. "I am so sorry, clinic was running really late. How did it go?"

"Fine." I threw my bag in the back of the car and climbed in. Paige was asleep in the front seat. I slumped in the back and pulled my hat lower so it covered my eyes.

"Did you win? How'd you do?" Mom asked quietly as she turned the car out of the lot.

"We won," I said flatly.

"I'm really sorry we missed it, Bry."

I couldn't believe my family had missed my first-ever home run. I didn't want to share the news; my anger felt like it completely overshadowed my excitement and pride. I shouldn't have to tell them about it. They should have been there to see it.

# Chapter 22

# IVs and Ice Cream

The next Wednesday was a teacher in-service day at school, a.k.a. a half day. Normally that would be awesome; practice is canceled if we have a half day, so usually we would all go hang out together at someone's house for the afternoon. But no, not me. Mom thought it would be a good idea for me to see what Paige goes through at clinic, and that maybe Paige would want company. Mom promised it was just an appointment for labs and a quick check-up and shouldn't take all afternoon. She promised that we would do something fun after Paige's appointment, my choice. I could tell that she still felt guilty for missing my game last week. As we pulled into the hospital parking lot, I had my headphones in and was slumped down in my seat in the back. I'll admit it: I was grumpy and wasn't going to hide it.

The clinic was near the entrance so we didn't have to go through the crazy maze like when Paige was inpatient. Mom checked in and talked with the woman at the desk. She said something about Paige's central line not working and her needing to get a poke. Paige sat down in a chair in the waiting room and started texting on her phone. I kept my music turned up as I sat down next to her. I watched a little boy, about two years old, running around the clinic waiting room flying a little toy airplane. He was bald, like Paige. While part of me felt really sad thinking about such a little kid being so sick, I also realized how accustomed I was getting to seeing people without hair.

"Paige?" We had been sitting for about ten minutes when the nurse called Paige back to the lab.

"I hate this part," sighed Paige. She looked nervous. We got into the room where they drew blood. Paige sat in the chair and Mom and I stood on either side of her. The nurse got the needle ready and put on a pair of gloves.

"I'm putting this big rubber band, the tourniquet, around Paige's arm to make her veins easier to find," said the nurse. I guessed she could tell this was my first time.

Paige's eyes got bigger and she took a deep breath in and held it. I tried to distract her with the first joke that came to mind. "Hey, Paige. What's the difference between roast beef and pea soup?"

"What?"

"Anybody can roast beef, but not everyone can pee soup!"

Paige smiled a bit and the nurse chuckled as she got ready to put the needle in.

"Want me to count?" the nurse asked.

"Sure," Paige said, grabbing Mom's hand.

"Okay...one, two, three...little pinch."

Paige let out a little gasp as she squeezed Mom's hand, but didn't move a muscle.

I tried to remember another joke to distract Paige while the nurse filled the syringe with blood and put it in several tubes. The blood looked a lot darker than I expected. I have always hated needles; I had to admit I was pretty impressed to see my baby sister being so strong. The nurse turned to me as she bagged up the tubes. "So, we'll send these to the lab for them to check her blood counts."

As we walked out Mom said, "They need to get the results back before the doctor sees her. It takes about 45 minutes usually."

I zoned out again and listened to my music for about a half hour until Paige's name was called by a nurse whose badge read *Maria*. She had long, dark hair and big brown eyes. She grinned as she walked towards us.

"Hey Paige, how are you doing today?"

"I'm okay," Paige responded. "This is my brother, Bryce."

I took one earphone out of my ear and smiled at her, trying to be polite despite my annoyance about being there.

"I haven't seen you here before, Bryce. Is this the first time you've been here with your sister?"

"Yeah, Mom thought that it would be good to see what kind of torture my sister endures while she's here." Maria laughed, catching on that I was joking around.

"Well, the first thing we do is her vitals. Not too much torture involved with that. We take her weight, height, blood pressure, and temperature. We need to make sure that her body is doing okay from the chemo."

Paige was obviously used to this, because she took off her shoes and sweatshirt before she even started. The nurse chatted with Paige as she took her vitals, asking Paige about school and weekend plans. She then put us in an exam room and we waited some more. Paige pulled out a deck of cards and we played rummy. I knew that hospitals were boring, but we had done more waiting today than anything else so far. At least I was finally able to beat Paige at cards before the doctor knocked and came in.

"Hi-ya, Paige. How are you feeling today?"

"I'm doing all right, Dr. Z. No pain or throwing up all week!"

He turned to Mom. "Is this true?"

"Yes, it's been a good week! I think we finally have her medications right."

The doctor smiled at me. "Who do we have here?"

"That's my brother, Bryce."

"It's great to meet you, Bryce. I'm Dr. Z. Is your sister behaving herself?"

I laughed, somewhat surprised by the question. "Well, if by behaving you mean making herself the ruler of the house and driving me crazy, I'd say she is doing just great!" Paige smacked me.

For as much waiting as we did before Paige's appointment, her actual visit with the doctor seemed pretty short. As we left, Paige begged Mom to stop for ice cream.

"I promised Bryce that it would be his choice what we do after your appointment."

"But Mom, I was the one who just had to get poked!" Paige protested.

"You did, and you did great, but I promised Bryce."

Paige turned to me, giving me a big smile. "Bryce, doesn't some cold, creamy ice cream sound just heavenly right now?"

I snorted and rolled my eyes. "It's fine, Mom." Under my breath I added, "It's all about Paige anyways, right?"

Paige looked at me sharply. "What was that, Bryce?"

"Nothing."

Mom just laughed, oblivious to the fact that I was annoyed. "You and your ice cream cravings, Paige!"

Waiting in line at the ice cream shop, I was making the very difficult decision between chocolate chip cookie dough and peanut butter swirl when I overheard a girl behind us in line laugh as she asked her mom, "Why is that boy wearing a skirt?"

Her mom looked embarrassed, shushed her daughter, and backed up a little. I didn't know what to say. I couldn't believe she had said that, right in front of my sister. I felt so bad for Paige. I looked over at her and her cheeks were a little pink and she was looking down at the floor. As we walked out with our cones piled high with ice cold deliciousness, Paige looked at me and rolled her eyes. "I hate it when that happens."

"That's happened to you before?"

"Oh yeah, I get all sorts of comments. Kids ask why I shaved my head, if I'm a boy or a girl, or what's wrong with me. And they stare and point at me or make mean comments like I can't see or hear them! Adults just look at me with this sad, frowny face, like they feel sorry for me, and I hate it. Why do you think I was so worried about going back to school?

I felt bad—I should have said something to that girl. It's my job as her brother to protect her and stand up for her. Paige seemed focused on her ice cream, but that stupid comment was all I could think about now. People could be so clueless and mean.

I didn't say anything more about it, but felt a little distracted on the ride home. Paige and I played video games for a while. We had a late dinner since we were all full from our pre-dinner dessert. As I helped load the dishwasher, Mom asked, "Bryce, before you make plans for the weekend, remember you have that Connect group, okay?"

"Yeah, I know." I was actually looking forward to going tomorrow. In a weird way, it was nice to spend some time with kids who actually got what my life was like.

## Chapter 23
# Bad Hair Day

"Hey, Bryce! Good to see you again," Kevin said, walking up to me.

"Hey!" It was so much easier being back in the group now that I recognized some people. I spotted Chris hanging up his jacket and walked over to talk to him while the rest of the group filtered in.

"All right, everyone. Time to get started!" Kevin was doing a last check of his sign-in sheet. Satisfied that everyone had shown up, he made his way to the center of the room.

"Good to see everyone!" Kevin said as we all sat down. "As usual, we have some new people, so let's start with introductions. This time, when you introduce yourself, please tell us your name, what your sibling has, and one thing you'd like to share from the past few weeks. Bryce, why don't you start us off?" I made a mental note for next time not to sit directly across from Kevin so I didn't end up going first all the time.

"Okay. I'm Bryce and my sister Paige has cancer. And...well, we were getting ice cream yesterday and someone thought my sister was a boy just because she was bald. I kind of wanted to turn around and snap at the girl, but I didn't want to embarrass my sister more than she already was." I hesitated, then added, "But then I felt really bad that I didn't say anything to stand up for her."

Hailey, who was usually pretty quiet, raised her hand.

"I've been with my brother and people have literally pointed and stared at him. It's so annoying. Walking around bald must be bad enough, but that's just rude to point at someone and whisper."

I was surprised to hear her get so fired up about something.

"The first time I heard kids make fun of my brother, I yelled at them and made fun of them back," Hailey continued, surprising me further. "My mom saw it happen and got a little upset with me. She reminded me that the kids were probably making fun of my brother because they didn't understand why he was bald. Sure, some kids can just be mean, but most likely they just didn't get it. She said I would get a lot better reaction if I calmly told them why my brother is bald. The next time it happened I looked the kid straight in the eye and very calmly told him my brother has *cancer* and the chemo makes his hair fall out. That shut him up pretty quick! I could tell he felt bad... which was good! The other time it happened I made a joke about my brother having a really bad hair day." She smiled shyly as everyone burst out laughing.

This group was definitely growing on me. After we finished introductions, we took a break to have some pizza, and I sat with Hailey and Chris. Chris and I were talking about the upcoming MLB season when I overheard Hailey ask Kevin, "Hey, where's Cat today?"

Kevin took a breath before answering, and I stopped mid-sentence to listen for his response. His face was serious as he replied, "I was going to talk with you all after lunch about this. Cat's brother died last week."

I felt my heart sink. My throat was dry. I thought I might throw up. Hailey had tears in her eyes and I looked away, thinking I might start crying too. Everyone sitting close who had heard the news was silent.

I had managed, for a while, not to think much about that particular worry in regards to Paige, although I knew it was always there in the background, threatening to overwhelm me. Now, the fear I had been pushing aside flooded to the surface. At the same time, I felt awful for Cat, imagining what she must be going through right now.

I vaguely heard Kevin talking quietly to the group. "You all know that your brothers and sisters are fighting different battles, with different kinds of cancer. This hospital is the best place they can be, and the treatment kids are getting these days has such a high success rate to cure cancer. This is the worst news to hear, not only because we all care about Cat and feel so sad for her and her family, but I know it also hits way too close to home for you all as you worry for your own family. I thought we could work on a project to send some love Cat's way, and if you want to talk about how you're feeling about this news, we can share that with each other too."

I didn't want to talk about it, but I quietly helped with the poster we made for Cat as my mind raced in a million directions. I could not imagine my family without Paige. She could *not* die. Our family would never be okay without Paige in it! I felt my heart beating frantically in my chest. I wanted to *do* something to make it not happen. But the knowledge that there wasn't anything I *could* do made me feel so helpless and...angry. This made me want to cry even more than the sadness that overwhelmed me: my sadness for Cat, my sadness at just the thought—the possibility—that this could happen to my family too.

I wasn't hearing the quiet conversation around me anyways, but I suddenly stood up and walked out, without looking back. I sat outside the room and stuck my headphones in my ears, the music blaring so loud it made my ears hurt. I just wanted to tune out the thoughts swirling in my head. Kevin came out to check on me but I shut my eyes tight, hoping he'd leave me alone. He put his hand on my shoulder for a few moments, and squeezed, but then left me alone, to my relief.

# Chapter 24

# Bowling to Baldness

"Honey, you're going to be late if we don't get going!" Mom shouted up the stairs.

"I don't feel like going, Mom." I was supposed to go bowling with Tyson, Luis, Kelsey, and Becca, but I just didn't feel like hanging out. On Friday nights the alley does black light bowling. Normally I love to go, but tonight it felt like it was going to take too much energy to socialize, especially since I'd been missing out on so much and would probably be reminded of it a hundred times. Plus, there was that ache in my gut that had been there since I'd heard the news about Cat's brother, and it was hard to focus on anything "normal," much less go and try to pretend to have fun.

"Honey, you're going. First you complained you could never do anything. Now your friends invited you and you don't want to go. What's up?"

"Nothing, I just don't feel like going, that's all." I hadn't said anything to my mom after group. How could I tell her something like that, and make her more worried and sad than she already was?

"Well, I ran into Ty's mom at the store today, and she mentioned how excited Tyson was to have you finally come over and spend the night. So come on, get in the car."

"Ugh, fine!" I threw a few overnight things in my bag and slowly made my way downstairs.

Mom and I drove to Ty's so I could drop my stuff off. Then Ty and I ran back to the car so she could drop us off at the bowling alley. When we got there, Luis, Kelsey, and Becca were already lacing up their rented, beat-up bowling shoes. Kelsey gave me a huge smile and handed me a pair in my size. Tyson looked at Luis and Becca. "Well, who has my shoes all ready for me?" He snorted, shaking his head as he headed up to pay for his own.

"Thanks, Kels."

"Bryce, I feel like I haven't seen you outside of school in forever!"

Becca chimed in, "Yeah, did you drop off the planet for a while or what?"

"I know. Things have been crazy lately. This whole cancer thing has pretty much turned my life upside down."

Becca turned and started laughing at something Luis said behind her. Kelsey asked quietly, "How are you holding up?"

"Me?" I was so used to being asked how Paige was doing; it took me a minute to think about how to answer. I smiled. "I'm doing okay. It kinda depends on the day. How Paige is doing seems to determine how we're all doing."

Luis was busy typing our names in for scoring. Kelsey and I walked over to choose balls. When we got back, it was her turn to bowl. I sat next to Tyson, who was inhaling a bowl of ice cream. It reminded me again of what had happened the other week at the ice cream shop. Suddenly, I remembered my accidental promise to shave my head when she lost her hair.

Kelsey sat down on the chair next to me on the other side. "Whatcha thinking about?"

"Oh, I just remembered that I'd kinda told Paige I would shave my head when she lost her hair. My dad did his, and I kind of avoided it and Paige didn't say anything. But—I think maybe I should do it." I told her about what had happened at the ice cream shop. "Do you think I would look weird bald?"

Tyson chimed in, "I'll do it with you, Bryce!"

I looked over at his big grin. "What?"

"Yep, let's do it tonight. We'll have Kelsey and Becca do it for us." He jumped up and grabbed his ball for his turn. He turned, raised his eyebrows, and looked at me, rubbing the top of the ball. "This is how we will look by the end of the night, Bryce."

Kelsey smiled at me and said, "Paige'll love it, Bryce."

Sure enough, when we all got back to Ty's house later that evening, he got his dad's electric razor from upstairs and the girls got to work on making us bald. Tyson insisted on going first. Once the last bit of hair fell onto the towel he rubbed his head and exclaimed, "Aerodynamics, Bryce! We'll be even faster around the bases without that hair to slow us down!"

I started to shake my head as I laughed at him, but Kelsey said, "Bryce! You've got to stay still! Sharp object on your head." I felt the vibration of the razor as she ran it carefully over my head, then the strange coolness without the warmth of my hair. Tyson wrapped his arm around my shoulders and turned me to the mirror. My eyes widened in shock, but I couldn't help but smile at my friend. Things may have changed a bit through all this, but when it came down to it, Tyson always had my back.

Kelsey grabbed my phone and took a picture of us to send to Paige. Paige texted back *OMG! You guys r the best. Luv it!*

## Chapter 25
# Life Carries On

When I got home on Saturday, I expected to hear Paige running up to the door to check out my head, but I didn't hear or see anybody. I closed the door, threw my bag down, and walked into the family room. Paige was sound asleep on the couch, the volume on the TV turned up so I could hear her celebrity gossip show blaring, giving us the latest details about the all-too-important lives of movie stars. Rubbing my head, I looked at Paige and noticed how small she looked lying there. I guess I hadn't really let myself think about how much she had changed since she started treatment. I was used to her bald head, but I hadn't really noticed how skinny she had gotten now that the steroid puffiness was gone, and how pale she looked.

I turned the volume down on the TV, then headed into the kitchen. Dad was sitting at the table with a mug of coffee and the paper.

"Hey, Dad!" I said as I headed to the refrigerator. I opened the door and peered in, hoping it was stocked with something I wanted to snack on.

I was interrupted by a surprised laugh from Dad. "Bryce! Lookin' good, bud!" He smiled as he walked up to me and rubbed his hand over my bald head. I grinned back at him. "Did you have a good time at Tyson's?"

"Yeah. Ty shaved his head too!"

Dad smiled even bigger, rubbed my head again, and grabbed his coffee mug for a refill. I closed the door to the fridge and grabbed some trail mix from the pantry instead. "I'm going to head up to start on my homework."

"OK. Mom's at the store. She should be back soon."

I grabbed my backpack and headed upstairs. Time to focus. The last thing I wanted to do on a Saturday was homework, but I was behind in a few different subjects and more than a little stressed about the upcoming math test scheduled that week.

I unloaded my backpack on my bed, throwing the heavy math and science books to one side and opening up my notebook to remind myself of my homework assignments. I sighed as I spotted the last math assignment I'd gotten back, scratched up with red to point out all my errors. "SEE ME" was written on the top of the page. I was officially lost. Math had always been a challenge for me, but algebra was ridiculous. Mixing up numbers with letters brought me to a whole different level of confusion. And lately trying to focus in class was nearly impossible. I was tired, distracted, and once I started to get behind I couldn't catch up.

I sighed again, and pulled out the homework that was due on Monday. I picked all the chocolate chips out of the trail mix to eat first, staring blankly at the paper as if the answers might magically appear on the page in front of me. They didn't.

Finally, after I'd eaten all the raisins and still hadn't tackled even one math problem, I closed the book in disgust and flopped onto my bed. I grabbed the book we were reading for Language Arts and started to read. I'd try math again tomorrow.

## Chapter 26

# Cancer Sucks

On Sunday night I woke up to hear my parents' mumbled voices and Paige crying. Was I dreaming? I blinked my eyes and rubbed my hand over my stubbly head. I reluctantly got up and saw the light on in the bathroom. Paige was sitting on the floor crying, with her head tipped up and blood streaming out of her nose and onto a wad of tissue Mom was holding. She looked pasty and pale, and her raccoon eyes were back again.

"What's going on? Is she okay?" I said, squinting in the bright light.

"She's fine, Bryce, just a little nosebleed and a fever. We're taking care of it. Why don't you go back to bed, buddy?"

"Um, okay." Feeling like they just wanted me out of the way, I turned around and stumbled back to my bed. I had a hard time falling back asleep because I was worried about Paige, but I must have drifted off somehow because the next thing I knew, light was streaming through my window and my alarm clock was going off. I got up and peeked into Paige's room to see if she was okay, but no one was there. I looked into my parents' room. No one there either.

"Bryce?" Kelly's voice yelled from the kitchen.

I ran frantically downstairs, afraid that something horrible had happened.

"Where is everyone?!"

"Your parents had to take Paige to the emergency room last night. They don't want you taking the bus because of all the germs so they asked me to come take you to school."

"The emergency room! Is Paige okay? Why didn't they wake me up to tell me they were going?"

"Paige is fine. She needed to get a blood transfusion and she has a little infection. They are giving her some antibiotics to help her body fight it off. One of your parents will pick you up from school."

"That still doesn't explain why they didn't wake me up to come with them!"

"Bryce, believe it or not, your parents are *trying* to keep some things normal around here. They knew it wasn't anything terrible, so that's why they let you sleep. They wanted you to go to school today and not be completely exhausted."

"Are you sure Paige is okay?"

"Yes. You know I wouldn't lie to you about this."

I poured cereal and milk into a bowl and sat down to eat. I stirred my spoon around the bowl, but didn't take a bite. My rice cereal wasn't crackling anymore by the time I got the courage to speak up.

"Kelly...can I ask you something?"

"Of course! You know that you can talk to me about anything...well, except baseball, I suppose," she added with a grin. Kelly had never been much of a sports person.

"Is Paige going to be okay?"

"Oh, yes, Bryce, it's just an infection. It happens."

"No, not like is she okay now. But is she going to be *okay*. As in get better?"

She stopped and put her arm around me. "That is the big, scary question that all of us worry about. But she's in a great hospital, with brilliant doctors who are giving her the best medicine...." Aunt Kelly looked at me and I thought she could tell I was not overly excited about her answer. I had heard a variation of this answer from too many people, and it never answered the actual question. She stopped and said quietly, "You just wanted me to give you a 'yes'?"

I felt worn out as I looked at her and said, "I just want to know it's all going to get better and I'll get my family back at the end of all this craziness."

She sighed. "Bryce, if I had a crystal ball I would love to be able to tell you that yes, everything will get better and go back to normal eventually. But the truth is, I don't know what's going to happen. None of us do. So far, Paige's body is responding really well to the treatment, and we have to focus on that right now."

"I know, I know. It's just hard. Not knowing. Waiting. And it *could* happen. My friend—from that SibConnect thing—her brother died."

She hugged me tight. "Oh, Bryce..." She stopped and took a big, slow breath. Then she leaned back a bit to look me in the face. I couldn't keep the eye contact, though, especially seeing the threatening gleam of tears in her eyes. I looked down at my hands as she continued. "How I wish I could promise you that will definitely not happen. I'm sorry that I can't." She gripped my shoulders tighter. "But I can tell you that I truly believe in my heart she will be okay. Cancer...is a big thing to fight. But you know your sister, Bryce—that girl is a fighter." The gleam in her eyes was different as she said this, a mischievous spark that reminded me of Paige's fiery side.

I couldn't help myself. I blurted out, "Cancer sucks!" Well, there it was. I couldn't really make it blunter than that, huh?

Kelly widened her eyes, and smiled. "Yes, it does. Cancer totally sucks. It's really changed things a lot, hasn't it?"

From there I just couldn't stop; the words tumbled out. "I miss out on almost everything with my friends, Mom and Dad bicker all the time, Paige gets whatever she wants, they forgot me at baseball practice, and my whole life is just different!" Wow, did it feel good to put that out there.

Kelly sat in silence for a minute. "Wow. Have you talked to your mom or dad about any of this?"

"No, I don't want them to worry about me. They are stressed out enough as it is. Plus," I mumbled, "I feel bad complaining, because I'm not the one with cancer."

"Bryce. Cancer sucks...and not just for Paige."

I looked at her, not sure what I wanted to say, but I couldn't stop the words from coming. "It just seems like I'm always an afterthought now." I felt the tears start to come and couldn't stop them.

"Bryce, I hope you know how important you are. Not just to your mom and dad, but to all of us. Paige being sick...it has put a strain on our family, and I know it seems like your parents are focused more on her. To a certain extent, it has to be that way, at least a little. Cancer is a serious thing—I know you are aware of that. Your parents are scared, and it is heartbreaking to see your child sick and not be able to fix it. More than anything else, they want Paige to get better...they want your family to go back to normal again, too."

I felt the tears coming harder now. Kelly still held my shoulders, but she pulled back a little to look at me. "Bryce, your mom and dad still love you just as much as before Paige got sick. They may not always have the energy they used to have to show you that all the time, and you are absolutely right—that is not fair to you. But it certainly does not take away from how much they love you! Your dad was just telling me the other day how amazed he is by your patience with Paige, even when she's being snarky, and I couldn't agree more. It has got to be really hard when you feel like you're fending for yourself when your world has turned upside down."

By this point, I had stopped crying. I used my sleeve to wipe my eyes. I felt so relieved that Kelly actually got it. She put her hand on my head and rubbed it gently, her eyes glistening a little.

"Bryce, ever since this first happened, I have seen you try to protect your parents from any additional stress, but that isn't your job. It is absolutely okay for you to talk to them about how you are feeling. It would be good for you and for them to get it out in the open. It won't change things back to how they were before, but it could be a step towards making things a little easier for all of you."

I felt like a weight had been lifted off my shoulders. I didn't cry very often, but I felt better than I had in a while. I also felt a little exhausted.

"And Bryce," she added, "I am *always* here for you, no matter what." She hugged me again, tight, then said with a smile, "It's a good thing you don't have a lumpy head. You look pretty cute bald, you know!"

A sudden, random thought came to me and I groaned.

"Okay, not cute. You look handsome."

"No, it's not that. I forgot to do my math homework; I just remembered. You know how you just said you were always there for me?"

"Nice try, Bryce." She kissed the top of my head. "I can write you a note, but you are going to have to talk to your teacher."

"I know, I know...I'll figure things out." Maybe if I kept saying that, it would actually happen.

Chapter 27

# Yet Another Let Down

The next night, Paige was still at the hospital. Dad and I were on our own for dinner. I walked into the kitchen and peeked in the oven: frozen pizza again. I used to beg for frozen pizza—not anymore. I was really starting to miss the days when I'd walk into the kitchen at ten in the morning and already smell Mom's chicken soup cooking for dinner that night. I could even have gone for one of those taco salads she makes to get extra veggies into us. I took a few slices into the family room, and began to eat on the couch while watching the game. Dad never used to let us eat in front of the TV. He always made a big deal about how important family dinners are. And ever since we were little, Mom has made us all go around and share our "best and worst" moments of our day. I used to roll my eyes about it sometimes, but now, I found that I missed it.

Dad was immersed in the spring training game on TV, and I realized how close we were to the home opener. "I can't believe the game is next week already! Ty and I have a plan for how we'll get on the Jumbotron this year. And I have a bet going with all the guys that I'm going to catch a foul ball. We gotta stay after the game to see if we can get some of the players to sign it."

Dad swallowed his bite and looked over at me with a crease above his eyebrows, never a sign of good news. My heart sank a little as I wondered what he was about to say.

"I've been meaning to talk to you about that, Bryce. I know how much you're looking forward to Opening Day, but I don't know if I can make it this year. I have a big meeting at work the day after the game that I have to get ready for. I have taken too much time off of work lately, and I just don't know if I can leave early again to make it to the game."

My heart dropped all the way into my stomach. I had been looking forward to some time with Dad, and getting away from the craziness of these past few months since Paige got sick. I felt like crying, or screaming at him. I turned my eyes down to my half-eaten pizza.

I opened my mouth to say I understood, but shut it again because that would be a big, fat lie. This had been a tradition every year for as long as I could remember. And this year we had really good seats. I stood up and started to walk toward the kitchen with my plate. It was one night. He couldn't give up one night of work to hang out with me? I was quickly getting pretty angry.

"Bryce, I will be at your next game, though. We'll all be there..." I pretended like I didn't hear him.

"Yeah, right," I muttered under my breath. I wouldn't count on that. Then I headed upstairs to my room and halfheartedly worked on some homework.

## Chapter 28

# Breakdown

When I got home from practice the next day, I tossed my backpack on the floor and sat down on the couch to watch TV. Paige was passed out asleep on the couch next to me. She had gotten home from the hospital that morning. I grabbed the remote and changed the channel to *MythBusters*.

"Bryce!" Mom called from the hallway. "You know the rules: no TV until after homework is finished. And can you please not leave your backpack in the middle of the hallway?"

"Mom, Paige has probably been watching TV all day."

"You know the rules, Bryce. Homework first."

"UGH!" I stood up, kicked my backpack so it was even more in the middle of the hallway, and stomped up to my room.

"Bryce! Get back down here and..." Mom kept talking but I was too upset to really hear what she was saying. At this point I didn't really care.

I lay on my bed and stared at the ceiling. I thought again about Dad canceling on me for the game. I picked up a baseball that was sitting next to my bed and bounced it off the wall, caught it, and bounced it again. *Thump, thump, thump.* I knew Mom hated when I did that, which was probably why I kept doing it.

I heard Mom's voice behind my closed door. "Bryce, can you please come move your backpack?"

"Do it yourself." Yup, I was going to be in trouble for that one. I didn't care. *Thump, thump...*I bounced the ball a little faster.

"Bryce! What has gotten into you?" She opened the door and glared at me with her hand on her hip. I looked up at her briefly and then threw the ball toward the wall again.

She reached out her hand and caught the ball. "Excuse me. You better stop this attitude right—"

I interrupted, "How about you tell me how long I'm grounded for and skip the lecture so I can start my homework?" I was surprised at how good it made me feel to talk back to her. Somehow, I felt less angry the more I knew I was making *her* angry.

She stared at me, opening her mouth like she was ready to start shouting. Then she drew a breath and just watched me for a minute. "That's it. The Bryce I know doesn't talk like that. What's going on?"

"Nothing." I closed my eyes, wishing she'd just leave me alone.

"Really? Nothing, huh? Well, you don't act disrespectfully to your family, no matter what is going on in that head of yours. You think you rule this house now, since your dad and I aren't here all the time?"

I felt tears of anger prick the lids of my eyes, and snapped them open. I couldn't help the sarcasm as I said, "Oh, yes, I definitely rule this house. Yep, me, not Paige. It's definitely not Paige who gets whatever she wants, whenever she wants it. It's definitely me who everyone drops everything for no matter what's going on..."

I couldn't help myself. "Yeah, Mom, I rule the house. That must be why my family is never at my baseball games, and why I have to cancel plans with my friends because of Paige..." I felt myself run out of steam as I looked up and saw tears in Mom's eyes. I'd been shouting, but I sighed and quietly said, "Mom, I miss our family. I miss the way things used to be. I know Paige is sick, I know she needs you guys a lot...but I'm still here. I feel like everyone has forgotten that I'm part of this family too."

Mom stood there, looking sad, and I wished I could take it all back.

"Bryce..." she came over and sat next to me on the bed. She took my hand in hers and I didn't pull it away. "Bryce, I miss you too. Seeing Paige so sick is one of the hardest things I've ever faced. But not being able to be the mom I want to be for you—that's hard too. This is probably the worst time our family will have to go through; I certainly hope so, anyway. It's going to be a long road, but it won't be forever..."

She pulled me up and hugged me hard. She whispered, "I'm so sorry, buddy. I promise we'll try to be more mindful of what's going on in your life, too."

I knew she was upset but I couldn't help myself. I quietly said, "You guys missed my first home run."

She kept my shoulders in her hands but pulled back to look at me. Her mouth was open and her eyes looked bright with tears. I looked away. She didn't say anything for a moment. Finally, she said quietly, "Oh, Bryce. You didn't say anything...I didn't know..."

I didn't know what to say. I knew Mom felt bad, but I still felt mad thinking about it and wasn't quite ready to let it go. It was quiet for a few moments and I felt kind of awkward. Mom had a strange look on her face, a mix of what looked like guilt and sadness, but with a hint of a smile. I must have looked puzzled, because she quickly said, "Bryce, I can't believe we missed it. I...I really can't believe we missed it. You didn't tell us—you must have been really mad." She sighed, but then smiled as she said, "But, buddy...you got a home run!?" Her eyes sparkled a bit, and I felt my frustration recede a bit as my feeling of pride from that evening crept back in. "Wait until your dad hears. I know it's belated but...can we celebrate?" She looked at me hopefully.

I still had mixed feelings, but I nodded and found myself smiling a bit too. I followed her downstairs, looking for Dad so I could tell him the story of my epic hit.

## Chapter 29

# Defender

I knew our talk paid off when my family actually all showed up at my next game. Even Paige was there. As Tyson and I were warming up, I saw two guys out of the corner of my eye laughing and goofing off in the opposing team's dugout. I recognized them since this team was our biggest rival. Alex, their pitcher, had a wicked fastball that Tyson struggled to hit. Jesse plays first base and is their strongest hitter. They weren't my favorite people in the world, always so cocky. Unfortunately, they almost always beat us. Tyson gave them his best fierce, we're-gonna-beat-you-so-don't-even-try look.

As I was throwing my last few balls Alex strutted out of the dugout, his hat backwards, his curly black hair spilling out the sides. Jesse, even taller than Ty and about twice as thick, was right on his heels.

"Hey, Bryce, isn't that your sister?" Alex nodded toward the stands where my family was sitting.

"Yeah," I said, wanting to wipe the sneer off his face.

"How come she looks like a dude?" Jesse busted out laughing.

I stopped mid-throw. I looked at Tyson. His face was turning red. As I gathered my thoughts, Ty threw down his mitt and started walking towards Alex.

"You better shut that big mouth, Alex..."

My mind flashed to the look on Paige's face when that kid made that comment at the ice cream shop. It was awesome of Ty to step in to defend Paige, but I stopped him before he got in Alex's face. I did instead.

"Really, Alex? You think she just up and decided to shave her head so idiots like you could make fun of her? She's got cancer, and she's getting chemo, which makes her hair fall out. She doesn't particularly like being bald, and dumb comments from insensitive jerks like you don't help. She's going through enough already."

Alex just stood there with his mouth half open, his face bright red. I turned back to face Tyson, who grabbed his mitt off the ground. Tyson was trying to hide a smile, and I gave him a half-smile back. We both turned to walk away.

Jesse spoke first.

"Uh, sorry, Bryce. Jeez, we had no idea. I hope she's okay, man." Alex mumbled an apology and they walked away.

"Dude! Way to put them in their place!"

"Thanks for having her back, Ty."

"Hey, she's like a sister to me too, Bryce. That's what you do for family!"

# Chapter 30

# Opening Day

I was still pretty upset that Dad couldn't come to Opening Day, but I was determined to have a great time. I got to stay at Tyson's house the night before. We stayed up late reading all the predictions for the game and upcoming season online.

"That's crazy! I can't believe that reporter said we were going to have a losing season!"

"Relax, Bryce. He clearly doesn't know what he's talking about. When we're hosting our sports radio show, we will be one hundred percent accurate for every sport, every season."

Tyson and I were wearing our baseball caps and jerseys. As we ran out the door, we each grabbed our gloves so we could go for any foul balls that came our way.

"I am so catching a ball this year. You're gonna owe me ten bucks and a Coke!" We always made a bet in case one of us caught one, although neither of us had ever had the chance—yet.

"Good luck, Ty. I'll be pushing you out of the way if anything even comes close to our seats." I stopped suddenly when I looked out at the driveway and saw Dad grinning from the front seat of the car, Ty's dad next to him.

"Dad! You came!" I slid into the backseat and he turned around to smile at me.

"I just couldn't miss it, Bryce."

Tyson's dad had a parking pass that let us park right across from the stadium, which was awesome. We passed through the gates and each grabbed a free hat. I put it on over the hat I was already wearing.

"Oooh, very nice, Bryce. How will I impress all the ladies in the stands if I'm sitting by you looking like that? These hats are so lame! That logo for First Bank is bigger than the logo of the team."

Laughing, I took it off. I'd bring it home and give it to Paige, tell her she could add it to her rapidly growing hat collection. She'd get a kick out of that. We got in line for hot dogs and some kettle corn. There was a buzz of excitement in the air, the collective hope for a new season—could this be our year to make it to the World Series?

"It smells so good! I have been craving a hot dog since last season," said Tyson, licking and smacking his lips.

As we came out of the tunnel to our seats, I stopped to take it all in. The grass was bright green and I wondered for the millionth time how they mow in that cool diamond pattern. The sun was out and the smell of hot dogs and peanuts was everywhere. Ever since I was little, this stadium had felt like my home away from home.

Our seats were on the second level, but we were in the third row along the first base line, so our view was perfect. Tyson and I watched batting practice as the stadium slowly filled up. The stadium announcer went through the line-ups, and then some singer I have never heard of sang the national anthem. The crowd started screaming before she sang the last line. The singer looked proud, as if we were cheering for her, but everyone was just ready for the game to start.

"Play ball!" Tyson and I yelled at the top of our lungs when the first batter entered the batter's box. The season had officially begun.

The game was awesome. The right fielder made an incredible throw to get someone out at second base in the third inning. Our team was down by one until the sixth inning when we scored four runs to take the lead. We stood on our chairs and danced during the seventh inning stretch to try to get on the big screen. I almost fell off the chair laughing as Tyson turned around and wiggled his butt toward the field, but still we didn't make it on camera. Dad pointed to the screen and said, "Guess you guys can't beat that!" Two huge guys, bare-bellied with their stomachs painted *GO* and *TEAM* were dancing like crazy on the Jumbotron.

Ty and I were both laughing hysterically as we settled back into our seats to watch the rest of the game. Even though we didn't catch a foul ball, it was a great day.

# Chapter 31

# The Wish

"Hey guys, how was it?!" Mom asked when we came through the door.

Paige said, "We watched the game on TV and looked for you guys. Clearly you weren't crazy enough to get on camera." I was impressed that Paige made it through a whole game—she thinks it's boring to watch baseball.

"We should have made it on TV with these moves!" Paige laughed as I demonstrated the dance Tyson and I performed during the seventh inning stretch. Dad even did Tyson's part—right down to the butt wiggle—which had all of us laughing.

I sat on the couch next to Paige, smiling at the sound of her giggles. During moments like these, she just seemed like her old self again, and I barely noticed the bald head above the smile.

"So, Bryce," my sister said, her eyes gleaming. I looked at her suspiciously, wondering what she was up to. "One of the 'benefits' of having cancer"—she made air quotes with her fingers when she said "benefits" but still had that gleam in her eye—"is that I get to make a wish for something that I really want and this organization will try to make it happen!"

"Wow! That's pretty awesome. So what are you going to wish for?" I hadn't heard anything about this, but was happy that Paige was getting something to look forward to.

"Welllllllll," she said, dragging it out. "You can imagine it is a bit hard to choose one wish out of all the things you could wish for. I could go on a shopping spree in a limo, meet someone famous, have my room redone..." I laughed. How was she ever going to choose between those options?

"But," her face got a little more serious and her voice got softer. "I was thinking about how this cancer thing affects all of us, not just me. So I wanted to choose something that all of us could look forward to."

I looked at her with surprise, feeling my excitement rise. She continued, "You know how we have been trying to talk Dad into taking us to Atlantis?" I opened my mouth to speak and she quickly said, "Well, I have to choose something in the fifty states, so..."

"Paige, where are we going?!" I couldn't handle the suspense anymore.

"Hawaii!!"

My mouth dropped open. "*No* way..."

"And we get to swim with dolphins, Bryce! Remember how we saw that thing on TV about those resorts? The one we are going to has some awesome water slides, you can rent surf boards at the beach..."

"Paige! That is so awesome! When do we get to go?"

"Well, I want to be able to swim, so I have to wait to get my central line out. So, hopefully in the winter. It will give you plenty of time to get into shape for the beach," she joked. I swatted her playfully and then spontaneously gave her a big hug. Everybody started chatting all at once about all the fun we could pack into the trip. I figured by the time the trip actually came, we might need to stay an extra week to build in time for all the relaxing, playing, and adventures we wanted to squeeze in. And what a great way to celebrate Paige being finished with chemo.

Paige looked over at me with a giant smile. "Told ya I'd find a way to get us to one of those cool places. I apparently just needed to get cancer to get us there."

"I think I would have rather just not gone to Hawaii, then."

"Bryce, I'm kidding. But if I have to have cancer, at least we get something out of it."

"I guess. It's going to be awesome! Thanks for picking something we can all do, Paige. That was really cool of you."

"No problem. Now you just have to be extra nice to me."

"Oh, that's how it is, huh?" I said, smiling, as I walked towards the kitchen.

Paige asked, "Where are you going?"

"I need a snack, want anything?"

"Bryce!" she shouted.

"What?"

"Do not even *think* about touching my Fruity-O's!" Paige grinned as we both lunged towards the kitchen.

# Epilogue

The car moves in slow motion up the track—*click, click, click, click.* Tyson, in the car in front of me, shouts, "Here we go, y'all!" as we get closer to the top. Kelsey grabs my hand and squeezes. I look over at her and smile, noticing how her eyes are reflecting my excitement and nerves for the ride.

It's the first day of summer break. Here we are again, facing the Scream-roller. It feels like so long ago, that day right before our family life flipped upside down and backwards with the news of Paige's diagnosis. Looking back on these past few months, I really can see how much Paige's cancer diagnosis and treatment has been like a roller coaster ride for our family.

I hear Kelsey gasp as we get to the top. For a moment everything seems to stop, then the terrifying rush of going down so fast, only to lurch back up and turn upside down. Always, that momentary panic of feeling like you may fall out. Of course, Paige's cancer brought our family much more than just a moment of that feeling, and I wonder when—or if—it will ever fully go away for any of us. At the same time, we have also experienced some ups along with the downs.

One more loop, another rush of adrenaline, and my heart is still racing as the car begins to slow. And I guess that right now, this is how my family is feeling, too. Not yet back to normal, still a bit dizzy from the plunges and turns on the ride so far, but feeling more steady and not so out of control.

We are not off the roller coaster yet. There may be more twists and flips ahead that catch us off guard. But as Mom and Dad say all the time, no matter what happens or what changes, we will always be a family. Upside down or right side up, we'll get through this together.

# Note to Readers

When your brother or sister is diagnosed with cancer, not only is his or her world turned upside down—yours is, too. Siblings of cancer patients are often called "shadow survivors" because, in the chaos of the diagnosis and treatment, they often receive less attention than they used to from their parents or caregivers. They may feel left in the shadows during the whole experience.

While every sibling's experience is different, we hope that Bryce's story touches on some of the emotions that you may be going through. So, how do you take care of yourself and support yourself during this difficult and scary time? What can you do?

## Stay Connected

Much like Bryce's parents, occasionally your parents won't have a choice but to prioritize your sibling's needs. Often, when a kid is diagnosed with a serious illness like cancer, he or she is showered with gifts and extra attention. Rules can be more relaxed for the sibling who is sick, and yet sometimes it seems that the rules are even stricter for you. At the beginning of treatment it may not be as frustrating; however, as time goes on, this can get old very quickly.

Some kids and teens don't feel like they should tell their parents how they feel because of how much their brother or sister is going through. But don't underestimate how important you are, too. It is okay to make your needs known and let your parents know how you feel. Even when stressed, your parents want to hear about how you are doing, what is going on in your life, and what you need.

It might work to set up a time each week for a family meeting. With everyone's hectic schedules, it helps to set aside time to reconnect, go over the possible schedule for the week, and talk about how things are going. When there is an event coming up that you would like to attend, ask your parents in advance if they are able to take you. You could also have a family member or close family friend as a back-up to take you if something comes up with your sibling. Make time for special outings with your parent or caregiver so you have some one-on-one time with them.

# Talk to Friends

No one quite understands what you are going through. You may feel awkward, annoyed, or distant while hanging out with your friends. What is important to them may seem trivial to you at the moment. Your friends may not understand why it's hard for you to meet up, or why you aren't feeling like yourself. Some kids might tease you about having a sick sibling. Or blame you for the illness. You may even feel uncomfortable and "different" from your friends.

Although you may be tempted to try to keep to yourself during this time, try to stay connected to your close friends. Try really hard! It's important to maintain as much normalcy in your life as possible. Go out with your friends. Invite them over. Arrange a regular get-together or time to touch base every day. Your friends may really want to be supportive or help, but just do not know how. If your friends don't know the right thing to say, sometimes they won't say anything at all because they won't want to risk upsetting you more.

Unfortunately, you may have to initiate conversations. So try talking first with a trusted friend about what you are going through or if you're having a bad day. At other times, enjoy the opportunities to have a distraction with people who can make you laugh, so you can have a break from thinking or talking about serious things.

## Discuss Your Feelings

You may feel like your emotions are all mixed up and you have a difficult time describing what is going on. Just start talking (or writing in a journal, or however you prefer to express yourself). You may want to read a book about emotions to learn more. Remember, however you feel is completely okay and understandable. But keeping your feelings bottled up can cause you to be resentful; have difficulty concentrating on school, friends, and after-school activities; and can result in a big meltdown like Bryce had with his mom.

Seeing your parents so upset and stressed out all the time might make it seem that you can't (or shouldn't) burden them with anything else. However, it's important for you to have someone you can talk to if you are feeling worried, anxious, or just having a bad day.

Find that person. Know that you can talk with your parents or another trusted family member, a school counselor, or a close family friend. Many hospitals have child life specialists and social workers who are there for you to talk to. Don't bottle up your feelings or push aside your own needs. Your life is not on hold because of a cancer diagnosis in the family. Also, don't assume anyone else knows what you are thinking or feeling. Your parents or caregiver may not even realize that something is bothering you. The only way they are going to know for sure is if you tell them.

If your feelings become too strong or disruptive; if you have trouble sleeping, eating, or concentrating on school work; if you have trouble getting along with friends; or if you lose interest in activities you used to enjoy, it may be helpful to consult a licensed psychologist or psychotherapist. Talk to your parents or a trusted adult to refer you to a professional therapist or counselor.

## Deal With Guilt

You get to go to school, see your friends, and attend activities, while your brother or sister has to go to the hospital, take medicines, and miss out on seeing friends. Sometimes siblings feel guilty because they are healthy, they have their hair, and they don't have to take medicine that makes them feel sick. You're right! It's not fair that your sister or brother is going through something like this; it's not fair that anybody has to go through it. But you shouldn't be punished because you were the "lucky" one who didn't get sick. Cancer is not anybody's fault.

One of the best things you can do in this situation is validate your brother or sister's feelings when he or she is feeling left out or upset that life has changed so much. No guilt, no worries, just let your sibling know that you understand how they feel and listen to whatever your sibling is talking about. It's difficult to do this because you may feel like you need to say or do something to fix things or make the situation better. However, sometimes all you can do is listen and acknowledge that things aren't fair. Be there for your sibling in the moment. Some sick siblings like to be filled in on events they have missed and see pictures while others like to pretend the events never happened. When your brother or sister is feeling down about missing activities, try asking what he or she would prefer.

## Face the Future

As Bryce describes to his Aunt Kelly, it is really scary not knowing for sure what will happen because of your sibling's illness. Are you someone who likes to know details? Do you feel like you have a good understanding of your sibling's diagnosis, treatment, and prognosis? If you want more information, ask to go with your parents to the hospital and talk with a doctor, nurse, or child life specialist to have your questions answered. Sometimes kids hear bits and pieces of conversations, either from listening to a parent on the phone, or tuning in to half a conversation at an appointment. It's easy for your imagination to get carried away, and you may picture something much worse—or much different—than what is really happening. Rather than filling in the blanks yourself or searching online to try to answer your questions, get the real answers from people who know what is going on with your sibling. If you are not able to visit the hospital, ask your family to send pictures or video chat with you, so you can have a better idea of what is going on.

## Update Your School

Make sure your parent or caregiver, and you, are keeping in touch with your school about what's going on. It's important for your teachers to know why you may be distracted or having a harder time concentrating. Often, siblings feel like they need to take on more responsibility at home, especially if their parents are staying at the hospital or traveling for treatment needs. This may make it difficult to balance the demands of school and extra-curricular activities too. If missing school—or the stress and changes at home—have made you fall behind, connect with the school counselor or your teacher to come up with a catch-up plan. If you need to miss school, designate a classmate or two who can take notes for you, communicate about homework, and deliver projects to school for you if necessary. If you are struggling, don't keep it to yourself and hope to figure it out later. Ask for help from someone who can help you get back on track now.

## Seek out Support Groups

Although Bryce was skeptical about the SibConnect program at Paige's hospital, he ended up thinking it was cool to meet some new friends who could truly relate to his experience with his sister's diagnosis. Something like this might be helpful for you, too. Look to connect with other siblings where your brother or sister is getting treatment. Ask your parents, your sibling's doctor, or other support staff at the hospital. They will know about community programs such as SibShops, Gilda's Club, or other support resources through your hospital. SuperSibs! (http://www.supersibs.org) is another support program that is available to kids and teens no matter where you live.

## Start a Blog

Some kids like to be part of creating and updating a blog to keep people updated. It can get tiring having people ask the same questions all the time. You may feel like you are the spokesperson for the family regarding how your sibling is doing. It can be a relief to direct people to check out the blog instead. A couple examples of sites made for this purpose are CaringBridge.org and CarePages.com. There are also several sites such as WordPress.com and Blogspot.com where you can set up a free blog about anything you like.

By telling Bryce's story, our goal is to help you realize that what you are feeling is okay, and that other siblings are probably feeling the same way. We also know that talking about these feelings may be difficult, especially when your parent or caregiver may already be stressed out with everything that is going on with your brother or sister. Above all, know that you aren't alone. The feelings you experience aren't weird or wrong—the ups, downs, and backwards loops of this roller coaster are something anyone who has a sibling with cancer can understand.

# About the Authors

The authors share a passion for supporting patients and their families throughout the entire cancer journey. They consider themselves fortunate to be able to do this through their work at Seattle Children's Hospital. This dedication, combined with learning so much from the amazing families they have worked with through the years, motivated them to collaborate and create a relatable resource for siblings.

Julie Greves, CCLS, is a certified child life specialist at Seattle Children's Hospital. She has spent over ten years working with pediatric oncology patients and their families. Julie graduated from the University of Puget Sound with a major in psychology and has pursued additional education in parenting children through illness. Julie lives in Seattle with her husband and two young girls. Her family enjoys spending time outdoors and traveling together.

Katy Tenhulzen, CCLS, is a certified child life specialist who has had the opportunity to support pediatric hematology and oncology patients and families at Seattle Children's Hospital since 2002. She graduated from Colorado State University specializing in child life, human development, and family studies, and has pursued ongoing learning in the areas of behavior management and parent education. Katy lives in the Seattle area with her husband and three sons. Their family enjoys outdoor adventures (rain or shine), playing or watching every sport from soccer to golf, and are known to friends and family as crazy Seattle Seahawks fans.

Fred Wilkinson, LICSW, has been an oncology social worker at Seattle Children's Hospital since 2001. He received his masters in social work from the University of Washington, and pursued additional education on supporting people who have experienced psychological trauma. He lives in the Seattle area with his wife Cindy. Fred is an avid runner who loves cooking and travel in his off time.

# About Magination Press

Magination Press is an imprint of the American Psychological Association, the largest scientific and professional organization representing psychologists in the United States and the largest association of psychologists worldwide.